SNOOPING CAN BE

Books by Linda Hudson Hoagland
from Jan-Carol Publishing, Inc

SNOOPING CAN BE DANGEROUS
THE BEST DARN SECRET
SNOOPING CAN BE CONTAGIOUS
SNOOPING CAN BE DEVIOUS

SNOOPING CAN BE

Devious

LINDA HUDSON HOAGLAND

Jan-Carol
Publishing, Inc
"every story needs a book"

SNOOPING CAN BE DEVIOUS
LINDA HUDSON HOAGLAND

Published February 2014
Little Creek Books
Imprint of Jan-Carol Publishing, Inc
All rights reserved
Copyright © 2014 by Linda Hudson Hoagland
Front Cover & Book Design: Tara Sizemore

ISBN: 978-1-939289-36-0
Library of Congress Control Number: 2014933645

You may contact the publisher:
Jan-Carol Publishing, Inc
PO Box 701
Johnson City, TN 37605
E-mail: publisher@jancarolpublishing.com
jancarolpublishing.com

*This book is dedicated to
Mike and Matt, my sons*

DEAR READER

I am presenting to you the third volume of the *Lindsay Harris Murder Mystery Series*, in which you'll find Lindsay traveling down the difficult path of motherhood and the choices she has to make to return her family to normal.

Lindsay's life is somewhat based on my experiences as a legal secretary-assistant. Of course, Lindsay is a little more daring than I was.

In this volume, Lindsay must find her missing son, Ryan. Joined by her twin daughters, Emily and Ellen, and her dear friend Jed, Lindsay embarks on the adventure of locating Ryan—only to discover that *Snooping Can Be Devious*.

Yours truly,
Linda Hudson Hoagland

ACKNOWLEDGMENTS

Janie C. Jessee, my publisher, earns my gratitude for allowing me to continue this series. I love to write, and I thank Janie for encouraging me to do so.

Thanks to all of my writer friends who push me to excel in all of my endeavors. They are: Joe Tennis, Rodney Smith, Jack Rose, Addie Davis, and many others too numerous to mention.

I am grateful to the Appalachian Authors Guild, Lost State Writers Guild, West Virginia Writers, and Reminiscent Writers for allowing me membership into their groups. They each have participated in the growth of my writing skills.

INTRODUCTION

Try as she may, Lindsay Harris doesn't seem to be able to experience ordinary days.

The simple task of grocery shopping leads her into the ordeal of being a witness to an armed robbery during which there is a death.

Ryan, her eleven-year-old son, is being pulled into a web of trouble by his new friend, Brian.

Emily and Ellen, her fourteen-year-old twin daughters, are now teenagers and no longer interested in the daily activities of their baby brother.

Jed, a writer friend of Lindsay's, is there to offer comfort and help, for which Lindsay is grateful. Taking on the windmills of the world is a difficult task, and along the way, Jed helps her to fight and win each battle.

But now Ryan in missing, and the family plus Jed must find out why.

Chapter 1

"Mom, can I go to Billy's house?" asked Ryan, as he glanced up from his hand-held computer game.

"It's 'may I go?' And yes, but be home by suppertime," I answered as I ran around the living room picking up items that didn't belong there.

I didn't know much about this Billy kid, and I knew I should correct that, but not today. There was too much to do today. I had to do the laundry for the four of us, clean floors in the kitchen and bathrooms, pick up all over the house, and vacuum.

Somewhere among all of those chores I had to fit in grocery shopping and writing checks to pay bills.

"Ryan, tell your sisters to come in here before you leave for Billy's," I said as he started walking toward the hallway to his bedroom to grab a jacket.

"Emily, Ellen, mom wants you!" he shouted from outside of their bedroom doors.

"Thanks, Ryan, I could have done that," I said sarcastically.

"Whatever," replied Ryan as he entered his bedroom.

"Kids," I said as I shook my head in annoyance.

I heard the girls coming down the hallway towards the living room chattering like magpies.

"Change your sheets and bring me your dirty clothes, Ellen and Emily," I told them as I tried to shout above their chatter.

"Now?" both girls asked in unison. It was a twin thing I suppose.

"Yes, now—and hurry. I need to get the wash started," I said sternly to get them moving.

At that moment Ryan came busting into the living room with his jacket on and computer game in hand.

"Tell Ryan to change his sheets and bring you his dirty clothes," said Ellen.

"He already did, Ellen. Now, go get that work finished so you can have your day free," I said with a smile.

"Awwww, Mom," grumbled Ellen as she and Emily turned and left the room.

My daughters were teenagers, both fourteen years old. That fact should explain everything when it came to dealing with them.

Ryan was a 'tween,' meaning he was beyond being a little boy but not quite a full-fledged teenager. At the ripe old age of eleven, he and his buddies knew all there was to know about being middle-schoolers.

"Mom, we put everything in the basement. Is it okay for us to go to Nancy's house?" Emily asked excitedly.

"What's going on at Nancy's?" I asked.

"She got a new computer for her birthday. She wants us to see it and then play some games," answered Ellen. Again, it was a twin thing. If I asked Ellen a question, Emily answered, and vice versa.

"Be home before supper. Why don't your girlfriends come here?" I asked curiously.

"We don't have a new computer," they responded in unison.

"Duhhh," I said as I made my way to the basement to start the laundry.

2

Chapter 2

This was one of those days when I truly needed a break from motherhood. I loved my children with all of my heart, but I needed some 'me' time, and I couldn't imagine that happening anytime in the near future.

I was tired. That's all there was to it. I was tired. I worked hard at trying to maintain the life that we had, but I needed a breather, a few moments to rejuvenate and recharge my batteries.

Suddenly I was alone. The girls were at Nancy's house, and Ryan had gone to Billy's house. The housework was screaming for me to finish it, but all I wanted to do was laze around on the sofa and watch a movie or two.

The telephone started ringing. I walked over to check the caller ID on the display.

'Unknown' and 'Blocked' were words that made me angry. If either one of those words popped up, I refused to answer the call. If the caller left a message, maybe I would call back; but, if there was no message, I knew it was probably someone trying to sell me something or want me to participate in a political survey. This was an election year, and the politicians were crawling out of the woodwork.

This time the name 'JUSTIN HARRIS' appeared boldly on the display. Justin Harris, my ex-husband and the father of my children, seemed to materialize before me when I least expected it or least wanted to be bothered by his sudden desire to be a father again.

I was determined not to answer his call, but my curiosity got the better of me. I picked up the phone.

"Hello, Justin," I said in a not-so-nice tone.

"Lindsay, you could be a little more pleasant with your greeting," Justin said sarcastically.

"What do you want, Justin?" I asked as I tried to modulate my tone.

"I want to take my son fishing. Are you going to let him come with me?" he asked sweetly.

"No," I abruptly responded.

"Come on, Lindsay, think about it. Ryan needs a male influence in his life. You know that, don't you?" he continued in his sweet, cajoling tone.

"No," I said sternly.

"Be reasonable, Lindsay. He is my son, too," Justin continued loudly.

"I don't like to go fishing," I added.

"Good, you don't have to go. This would be a father–son thing. No women are allowed," he said with a laugh.

"No," I answered again.

"Lindsay, I want to take Ryan fishing," he yelled.

"You know what the judge said the last time you dragged me to court. You can visit the kids, at my house, with me present, and that's the only way you can see them," I explained angrily.

"Forget that judge. I want to take Ryan fishing with me," he demanded.

"I'm going to hang up now, Justin," I said as I placed the phone back on its cradle.

4

I thought that was a strange phone call because Justin was focusing on Ryan. There was no mention of his daughters. Of course, the girls were reaching a rebellious stage and openly expressing their feelings of their father.

Lately that had manifested itself in, "I want him to visit, once in a while, but I certainly don't want to live with him." Of course, they still loved him, but they preferred to do that from a distance.

I did not discourage their love for their father, but I, too, wanted him to love them from a distance.

Ryan loved his father, I think, even though he and his sisters had endured being stolen from me by their father and driven out-of-state to live with him.

The ordeal of being stolen had upset Ryan tremendously at the time, but now he saw it as his father wanting him enough to steal him from me. That had to be love, didn't it?

The phone call yanked me out of my lazy crave and directed me toward my motherly duties. Besides, I wanted to burn off the angry energy that had built up in my heart and soul.

I wondered what Justin was up to and what would happen in the near future.

I knew I had to keep an eye on Ryan.

Chapter 3

I ran to the basement to sort the piles of clothes that were on the floor. After shoving a big load of jeans into the washer, I turned it on and allowed it to do its thing. I returned to the living room, where I grabbed my car keys and grocery list. I had to buy groceries, or we were going to have soup and crackers for dinner. My cupboard was bare and in need of attention.

Since it was Saturday, the grocery store was full of weekly shoppers. Of course, I ran into many people I knew, all of them wanting to talk beyond a passing hello.

I marked each item off my list as I tossed it into the cart. I knew I had enough money to purchase what I had listed, but I couldn't go very far beyond the list.

I hadn't included snacks on the list for the kids, so I was wandering the aisles looking for anything that was on sale or at a reduced price.

Suddenly I heard a loud pop, that pulled me from my search for snacks. I glanced around, searching for the source of the sound. Then there was another pop, louder this time, followed by screams.

I froze.

I didn't know which way to move. I crouched down trying to hide myself behind my shopping cart so no one could see me from over the top of the aisle. Sometimes it paid to be short. This was one of those times.

I left my shopping cart standing and sneaked my way toward the front of the store where I had heard all of the commotion. I poked my head around the corner, slowly, cautiously, so I wouldn't get it shot off, because I realized that the pops were gunshots.

I could see a body on the floor, sprawled in a pool of blood. A man was standing over him kicking him to see if he were dead.

Other people were on the floor, but they didn't appear to be bleeding, and they were moving around a bit.

I pulled my head back and got down on my hands and knees. I offered a quick prayer of *Thank you!* that I didn't have my children with me and that I wasn't leading them into danger.

I crawled forward a bit to get a better view of who had been doing the shooting. He had to still be there because the other people on the floor weren't making any effort to stand up and make a break for the front door.

I crawled forward, like a fool, to get near the other people so I could blend in and not completely surprise anyone who might find me in the aisle.

I could see the shooter.

I could hear two gun-toting men running from cash register to cash register, shoving the contents of each drawer into two bags.

Then, I heard the third one—the shooter. He had moved into the office and was shouting at the store manager.

"Open that safe," the third robber shouted as he waved his gun around.

When I raised my head, I could see the office and the manager, who was scared to death.

"I will," the manager sputtered. "Just give me a minute."

I watched the store manager as he struggled with the combination lock. He turned it right—left—right and yanked the door.

Nothing.

He spun the combination wheel and started the process again.

Turn right—turn left—turn right, and yank. The door opened, and he fell over from the effort.

He started to get up from the floor, but the shooter crashed his gun butt onto his head. The manager fell over again with a thud.

I pulled my head back down so the robbers wouldn't see me watching them—all three of them.

I was trying to see their faces, but they were covered with rubber masks that fit completely over their heads, hiding even their hair. If you stared at them straight on, you might be able to determine the color of their eyes, but that was all.

The robber in the office came running out to where the other two were standing, having emptied the cash registers.

"Let's go!" he shouted.

I heard a noise. It sounded like an unusual ring tone for a cell phone. It was a faint tinkling sound. I thought it belonged to one of the people sprawled out on the floor.

I watched as all three robbers ran out of the front door and into the parking lot. I dialed 9-1-1 and told the dispatcher that the store had been robbed.

Chapter 4

"Can you describe the perpetrators?" asked the town policeman.

"They all wore masks—the kind that completely covered their heads, so all we could see was their eyes if we looked at them head-on," I answered.

"What kind of clothes were they wearing?" he asked.

"Jeans, both pants and jackets," I answered.

"What about their feet?" he asked.

"Boots, I think, but I'm not sure about that," I said, as I tried to picture them in my mind.

My mind was fogging up, giving me problems. I realized that the fear caused by what I had experienced was overtaking my need to be clear-headed.

"Are you all right, ma'am?" asked the town police officer.

"Yes, I think so," I answered as I tried to maintain control.

I had felt myself blanch. All the blood seemed to have left my face, leaving me pale, sickly, and white.

"Are you sure?" the town police officer asked as he stared at me.

I put my head down, took a deep breath, and exhaled loudly. The dizziness that I had felt was beginning to subside.

"Yes, sir," I said. "I think everything that has happened and could have happened just hit my brain. We all could have been killed."

"Yes, ma'am," he responded. "Do you remember anything else about the robbers?"

"No, sir," I answered honestly.

"My name is Bart Martin. Call me if you remember anything else that might help us."

"Yes, sir, I will," I said as he walked away from me and approached another person who had been on the floor with me.

I grabbed my handbag and left the groceries sitting in the cart. I would have to grocery-shop tomorrow. Tonight I was going to go to the Pizza Place and get a couple of pizzas for us to eat for dinner.

As I drove home to finish the laundry, I tried to unscramble my thoughts. Something about the robbery was prodding and poking at me, but I couldn't quite figure it out. *What was needling me?*

Chapter 5

When my children arrived home from visiting friends, I briefly explained to them that I had witnessed a robbery at the grocery store and that we were having a treat for dinner. I called the Pizza Place to have our food delivered.

"Mom, you're not in any danger, are you?" asked Emily, as she stared at me with wide eyes.

"No, why would you think that?" I asked. I really hadn't given much thought to it—the danger idea, I mean.

"Well, how many times have we seen television shows where they—the robbers or murderers, or whatever—are trying to eliminate the witnesses?" asked Emily.

"Those are make-believe stories, not real, Emily. Please don't worry, Em. Don't any of you worry. Okay, Ellen and Ryan?" I said as I tried to calm their fears, which only proved to bring mine to the forefront.

"What did they look like, Mom? Did they wear masks? Did you recognize any of them? How many were there?" asked Ryan excitedly.

"One question at a time," I suggested.

"Okay, did you recognize any of them?" he repeated.

"No, I did not. They were wearing masks," I answered slowly, as my mind flashed back to the scene.

"What kind of masks?" asked Ryan.

"Ski masks, so I could only see their eyes and mouths," I answered.

"You didn't recognize any of their voices?" asked Ellen.

"No, I don't think so. They really didn't talk very much. I'm sure they tried to disguise the sound of their voices when they did speak," I said.

"Did they talk like they were from around here? You know, people say we talk differently from other people. I don't hear a difference most of the time, but I can tell when someone who isn't from around here and is visiting. They sure do sound odd," said Ryan.

"Yes, Ryan. I think they were from around here," I answered.

"That makes it a lot scarier, Mom," said Emily.

"What do you mean?" I asked Emily.

"If they are from around here, you could run into them at any time. They could come after us to get to you, couldn't they?" said Ryan as he jumped into the conversation before I could answer the question.

Ryan was becoming frightened and truly agitated. Ellen and Emily moved a little closer to each other, seeking safety in each other's presence.

I watched my children take on the fears that I should have been feeling but wasn't. *Was there something wrong with me?*

There was a knock at the door.

"Pizzas are here!" Emily shouted as she opened the door.

"Here, come get the money," I shouted as I held up a twenty-dollar bill and a five-dollar bill.

Emily must have been distracted because she did not grab the money I was holding. Instead, she was staring at the delivery boy with her mouth open and her eyes sparkling.

12

His appearance was strikingly handsome. He was not what you would expect a pizza delivery boy to look like.

"Emily, pay the young man," I said as I tried to get her to stop staring.

"Okay, here's the money," she said as she took the two bills from my hand. "Keep the change."

I looked at her sternly, but it was too late. The pizza delivery boy ended up with a tip of over seven dollars.

After eating, I needed to get them to their rooms and out from under my feet so I could get some work done.

"All right, guys, there is absolutely no reason to be afraid. The police are investigating this and will make arrests some time soon. I know they will," I said as I smiled a wide smile. "Now, give me a big hug and go do something in your rooms so I can get this living room vacuumed."

The girls took off running. They were going to call all of their friends to tell them what happened to me.

Ryan walked slowly to his room, glancing back at me a couple of times. There was a pensive frown on his face and I could see unspoken questions forming in his mind.

How was I going to be able to convince Ryan that he wasn't in any kind of danger? Was that true? Were we in danger because I had happened to be in the grocery store when it was robbed, thus branding me as an eyewitness to a felony? Did Ryan think I had allowed this to happen? Wow, kids are complex!

Chapter 6

Bedtime finally arrived. We had endured what seemed to be a tremendously long Saturday, what with all of the worries brought on by my being an eyewitness to a robbery and murder.

Emily and Ellen spent the entire evening chatting with friends—on the phone and, of course, on Facebook. That was a normal Saturday night for them since they were not quite old enough for the dating scene and mall trips.

Ryan went into his room and closed his door, re-appearing only to go to the bathroom. I heard no sounds of any kind of entertainment coming from his room. He seemed to be brooding in the darkness.

Surely my involvement as a witness to a crime didn't cause all of the quiet darkness that filled his room and invaded his mind. There had to be another reason for the change in his temperament and personality. I was going to have to sit down with him and have a nice long and forced talk.

"Tomorrow. I'll do it tomorrow." I mumbled as I fell asleep.

***

"That's him! That's the killer!" I screamed as I pointed to a man standing in the center of a crowd of on-lookers.

Everyone in that crowd started looking at each other as they each looked for the person I was pointing out to the town police officers who were surrounding me.

Then he was gone. He completely disappeared, evaporated, melted away, as if he were an apparition, a ghost, a shadow in my mind.

"Where is he, ma'am?" asked a big, burly bear of a policeman.

"Gone," I whispered. "He's gone."

"Which way, ma'am?"

"He disintegrated," I said in disbelief.

"Which way, ma'am?" the officer asked again.

"I don't know," I whispered loudly, angrily.

That was all I could say.

The onlookers were becoming unruly, backing away from anyone they didn't know. This was a small town. The strangers should have been few and far between, but they weren't necessarily backing away from strangers. They were putting distance between themselves and neighbors who were friends, tossing accusatory looks at any male standing near them.

Suddenly, the crowd of onlookers was gone. I hadn't seen them disintegrate, fade away, or dissolve, but I knew that had happened.

Then I was alone.

Where had the police protection gone? Didn't they know that I was in danger? Didn't they know that the man I identified was going to kill me? Didn't they know who that man was?

I heard a gunshot. It bounced off of the pavement in front of me.

I looked for a place to hide. There was nothing. I was completely surrounded by pavement offering me no place to hide.

"Where are the buildings?" I asked, as I turned around and around with my eyes wide open, searching for a hiding place. There should have been cars parked along the street. Where were the cars? I could hide behind a car. "Where were the cars?" I screamed until I woke myself.

It was only a dream, but it had seemed so real. *What was happening to me?*

My bedroom door burst open, and my three children came running to my bed.

"Mom, are you all right?" asked Ellen. "Why were you screaming?"

"It was a bad dream, that's all," I said as I hugged them close to me. The hugging was getting harder to do with the passing of each day. My babies were becoming adults—well, almost adults.

The girls turned to go back to their rooms, but Ryan lingered. He was sitting on the edge of my bed, watching me.

"Are you okay, Ryan?" I asked, as I looked at his solemn face.

"Sure, why wouldn't I be?" he asked.

"Just checking," I replied. "Go back to bed, son. We need to get some sleep."

"Okay," he said as he stood up to leave my bedroom.

"You dreamed about the killer, didn't you?" he asked.

"Yes, but that was all it was, Ryan. It was only a dream," I said as I tried to settle his thoughts again.

"Good night, Mom," he said as she shuffled out of my bedroom.

"Good night, baby," I answered softly.

Chapter 7

"Who is up to going to church?" I asked as I stood in the hallway outside of the bedrooms filled with my children.

"I'm not," Ryan shouted with a loud, strong voice.

I heard only groans from the girls.

"Okay, okay. Go back to sleep. We had a rough night. I think God will let it pass this time," I said as I walked to my bedroom where I fell back onto the bed. I knew I wouldn't be able to go back to sleep. I had too much to do. After all, I had to go to work the next day. I had to be rested and ready for a day with Wayne Maxwell, Attorney at Law.

I heard the telephone ring, but I was sure it wasn't anyone calling me. It was probably one of Emily's and Ellen's friends. Ryan's friends wouldn't call this early on a Sunday morning.

The ringing stopped and no one yelled for me to pick it up, so I crawled out of bed again and tried to motivate myself to start my day.

When I saw Emily in the kitchen I asked, "Who was on the phone early this morning?"

"Don't know. Didn't answer it," Emily said.

"Did your sister answer the phone?" I asked.

"I don't know," Emily replied.

As if on cue, Ellen entered the room.

"Who was on the phone?" I asked Ellen.

"I don't know. I thought you answered it," she said with a shrug of her shoulders.

"I guess Ryan answered it," I said, as the girls gathered boxes of cereal for breakfast.

"You don't want a big Sunday breakfast?" I asked.

"No, I'm not that hungry," said Emily.

"Me neither," agreed Ellen.

The phone call was bothering me. I wanted to know which of Ryan's friends would have called so early in the morning.

I poured myself a bowl of cereal and enjoyed my cold breakfast while I waited for Ryan to make an appearance. Just as I was putting my bowl in the sink for washing later, Ryan entered the kitchen.

"Morning, Ryan," I said cheerfully.

Ryan groaned at me.

"Cat got your tongue, Ryan?"

"No," Ryan said sullenly.

"What's your problem, son? Who are you mad at? Why are you in such a mood?" I asked softly as I tried to get him to talk.

"Forget about it," said Ryan.

"No, I won't forget about it. What's the problem?" I asked sternly. "Oh, by the way, who called early this morning?"

"Why are you asking me?" he said with a startled look.

"I didn't answer the phone and neither did your sisters. Now, I want to know who called," I continued to probe.

"It was my father, okay?" he snapped.

"What did he want?"

"He told me you wouldn't let me go fishing with him," he said angrily.

"That's right, Ryan. I did say you couldn't go," I explained through gritted teeth.

"Why not? He wanted to take me fishing. What's wrong with going fishing? You won't take me, will you?" he snarled.

"Ryan, have you ever asked me to take you fishing?" I questioned my angry son.

"No, I didn't want to waste my breath. All you would do is tell me no," he continued, with a little less anger.

"Well, Ryan, when do you want me to take you fishing?" I asked sincerely.

"How about today, Mom?" he asked with sarcasm evident in his tone.

"You know I can't go today. Give me another date, a weekend, okay?" I asked.

"Forget about it," he said, leaving the kitchen without eating any breakfast.

"Get back here and eat, Ryan," I said loudly.

"Not hungry," he answered as he closed his bedroom door.

"I've got to figure out how to reach him," I mumbled as I walked to my bedroom to shower and dress for the day.

I picked up my phone extension in my bedroom, listened for the dial tone, but heard a whispered conversation instead. "Gotta go, Ryan. Someone else just picked up an extension," whispered a disguised voice.

"Bye," said Ryan, as he quickly hung up his receiver.

I left my room in search of an answer.

"Ryan, who was that on the phone?" I demanded as I rushed into his bedroom.

"Just a friend, Mom. What's the matter now?" he asked as he tried to control his voice.

"Who is this friend? What is his name?" I continued.

"Brian."

"Brian who?" I probed.

"I don't know his last name. I never asked, and he didn't tell me," said Ryan as he stared at his feet.

"Are you lying to me, Ryan?"

"No, Mom. He just said to say that his name is Brian if anyone asked," said Ryan.

"What does that mean?" I asked.

"What does what mean?" Ryan asked. It was as if he was trying to confuse the conversation.

"You know what I mean," I said sternly.

"He just said to tell anyone who asked his name is Brian. That's the truth, Mom," Ryan said to the floor.

"What did Brian want?" I asked.

"Nothing. Just to talk," he said.

"I didn't hear the phone ring. Did you call him?" I asked.

"No, when I picked up the phone to call Jason, Brian was on the line. I guess I picked it up before it had a chance to ring. Happens, you know," he explained to his feet.

"Yeah, Ryan, I know," I said, giving up on trying to pry anything out of him.

Ryan was not even a teenager yet, and I was getting the bad behavior long before I had thought I would.

It was actually hard for me to understand why he would want to spend any time at all with his father. Earlier in the year, all three of my children had been kidnapped by their biological father, Justin, who was the man with whom Ryan wanted to go fishing.

It appeared that Ryan had managed to forgive and forget. The girls and I had not followed suit.

Maybe I'll trust him someday. Just maybe.

Chapter 8

I got my brood off to school Monday morning without a hitch. That was a pleasant surprise, especially for a Monday. Now I was in a quandary. Who was I going to ask to help me get some fishing gear assembled? I had no clue as to what rod would be best for which kid.

"Lindsay, you have a call on line two," said a disgustingly cheerful voice over the intercom.

"Thanks, Anna," I said as I winced. I knew I didn't sound too friendly.

I looked at the caller ID and saw Jed's name appear.

"Hey, Jed," I said into the phone before he got a chance to say hello.

"Hi, Lindsay. I just wanted to touch base with you to see what's been going on in your area. What's new?" he asked.

"I haven't heard about anything that might be of interest to you or your newspaper. No news happening in Stillwell right now that you could write about in your human interest column," I said.

"I was hoping you had come up with something we could investigate," he said softly and then added a laugh.

"Sorry, but I do have a question for you," I said, as I tried to work up the courage to ask.

"What's the question?" he said.

"Do you fish?" I asked sheepishly.

"What?" he asked.

"Do you go fishing?" I whispered.

"I have fished, but it's been a while. Why do you ask?" he said.

"I need to buy some fishing gear for myself, my two girls, and especially for my son. I have no idea what I need, so I could use some help. I don't want a pushy sales guy selling me stuff I don't need," I explained.

"I know what you mean, and I'm sure that would happen. You know that this idea is going to cost you some money?" he asked sincerely.

"I know, but bonding with Ryan is worth it," I replied.

"What brought on this sudden desire to go fishing?" Jed asked.

"Ryan's biological father is trying to convince me that I need to allow him to take Ryan fishing. I can't do that. If Justin takes him anywhere, he won't bring him back to me. So I want it to be a family thing," I said.

"Let me take him fishing, just me and him. I'll find out if you really need to go to all of that expense," suggested Jed.

"I can't ask you to do that. I—"

"You didn't ask me. I'm asking you. What do you say?" Jed asked.

"That would be great. When?"

"Next Saturday. I don't have anything scheduled. I'll do it then," said Jed.

"Jed, I did remember something that might interest you," I said.

"What's that?" he asked.

"I witnessed a robbery and murder a couple of days ago," I whispered.

"Are you talking about that grocery-store robbery? Were you there?" he asked excitedly.

"Yes, I'm sorry to say I was one of those people who had to lie on the floor to keep from being killed," I answered.

"You're kidding." he asked.

"I wish I were," I responded sadly.

"What's happening now with the case?" he questioned.

"I don't know. No one has called me with more questions," I said.

"Why don't you call them?" he asked.

"I'm afraid to ask," I mumbled.

"Why?"

"I might have to tell them about the eyes," I whispered.

"Whose eyes?"

"That's it. I don't know, but I remember them from somewhere. If I ever see them again, I will know who the killer was," I whispered so no one could hear me other than Jed.

"Are you sure?" he asked excitedly.

"Absolutely positive."

"I need to take you out and about so you can find those eyes again," he whispered excitedly.

"I don't know about that," I said.

"Did you see any sign of recognition when he looked at you?" Jed asked.

"I'm not sure. I felt a connection, a link. I really don't know why. It was like seeing someone from your past and struggling as you try to remember who that someone is. Do you know what I mean, Jed?"

"Yeah, I think I do. You need to find out who from your past would or could be a killer," said Jed.

"I'm not sure I really want to know," I whispered, as I saw Wayne glare at me as he walked passed my office door. "Gotta go, Jed. Call me later, okay?"

23

"What time do you get off work?" he asked quickly.

"Five."

"I'll meet you at your house about that time," he said as he disconnected the line, giving me no chance to object.

As soon as I placed the receiver of the telephone into its cradle, Wayne crossed the threshold into my office.

Chapter 9

"What can I do for you, Wayne?" I asked cheerfully.

"Have you completed the paperwork for the Perkins Closing?" he snapped.

"Yes, sir, it's right here," I said happily, or as happily as I could be with Wayne's temper showing again.

"When were you going to tell me about what happened to you this weekend?" he asked wearing a facial expression of someone who had been hurt by another's words, or in my case, the lack of them. It was such a drastic change from his demeanor when he initially entered my office.

"I'm sorry, Wayne. You have been busy all morning, so I just didn't want to interrupt you. I wasn't trying to keep it from you. As a matter of fact, I wanted your help with what happens next," I explained sincerely.

"I should hope you would come to me for help. I would not want my legal assistant to go to another lawyer for advice that I'm perfectly capable to dispensing," he said, as he forced his tone to remain calm. It was a real struggle for him, and it showed.

"Okay, Wayne, tell me what, if anything, I need to do," I said.

"You're a witness and a victim, Lindsay. The Stillwell County Commonwealth Attorney will tell you everything, especially if the perpetrators are caught and they proceed to trial. You may not be able to do anything except answer questions posed to you by Mr. Jessee, the Commonwealth Attorney, who will add your statement to his file until action needs to be taken. An actual trial could be weeks, months, or years away with you just hanging fire until then," said Wayne.

"I didn't realize it could last so long," I said with a sigh.

"It can and most likely it will," Wayne said.

"All I can do is wait," I said as I sighed again.

"You aren't afraid, are you?" he asked.

"Should I be?"

"Did you recognize anyone who might have recognized you?" he asked.

"No, they wore masks," I said, as I tried to convince both of us that I was telling the whole, unadulterated truth.

"When the Commonwealth Attorney contacts you, let me know, and I will go with you to talk with him," suggested Wayne.

"Sure. Okay, Wayne," I told him as he turned to leave my office.

I pushed papers around my desk for a few minutes as I tried to look busy.

I walked to the front lobby where Anna was stationed at her reception desk.

"Do you want to go to lunch with me today?" I asked, seeking company. I truly hated to eat alone.

"Yeah, sure, but what about the phones?" Anna asked.

"I'll ask Everett to cover for us," I suggested.

"Good. I'd love to get a chance to go to lunch with you. We don't get to do it very often because of these silly old phones," said Anna as she smiled broadly.

"I know. That's why I think Everett will cover for us. He's a really good guy, you know," I said.

It took me a moment to ask Everett for his approval, then off we went to the only restaurant within walking distance to enjoy our rare lunch together.

"Anna, you said your dog died mysteriously a couple of months ago. Did you ever discover why he died?" I asked, showing a great deal of sympathy because I knew that Anna had truly loved that dog.

"No, I couldn't afford the necropsy—that is an animal autopsy—so all I had left was what I really believed deep down in my heart," said a solemn Anna. Her smile and the sparkle of happiness that had been in her eyes had totally disappeared.

"What do you think happened?" I asked knowing she really needed to talk with someone about this.

"I believe someone poisoned him. I don't know when or how because the only times my dog was outside, he was with me or in his fenced-in yard out back behind my house," she said as tears clouded her pretty, young face.

"Who do you think would do that?" I asked as I tried to pull more words from her.

"My neighbor," she answered quietly.

"Why?" I asked.

"He didn't like my dog, and he doesn't like me," she said and a rare spark of anger lit up her face.

"Why? You are one of the nicest people I know, and I'm sure your dog would have been just like you," I said, trying to help her get past her anger.

"He said my dog barked all the time and tried to bite him. If he did try to bite him, it was because he was teasing him. You know how stupid people can be when they see a fenced-in animal. They poke at them with a stick and try to make them angry enough to lunge at the fence. I've seen people do that, but I didn't ever catch my neighbor doing it. I wish I had, and then I would feel better about blaming him," Anna explained.

27

"You said he doesn't like you. Why?" I asked.

"I guess it was because of the dog. We have had no other contact about anything else. He said when I was at work, the dog barked all the time when he was outside, so I started leaving him in the house while I was gone. I put him outside only when I was home. He didn't bark very much when he was outside and I was home. So, I don't think he barked much when I was gone unless he had a reason to do so," said Anna.

"Lunch is here. Let's eat. I'm starved," I said as I hurriedly salted my fries and then covered them with ketchup. I took a couple of fries, shoved them into my mouth in a very unladylike manner, followed by a big bite from my cheeseburger.

"You really act like you're starved," said Anna as she watched me chew.

"I'm a stress eater, Anna. When I start to feel pressure along the home front, I eat. It's a good thing the stress at work doesn't trigger the eating, or I wouldn't be able to walk around with all of the pressure Wayne piles onto me," I explained between bites.

"What's all the home stress about?" she asked worriedly.

"We were talking about you and your dog. We need to continue with that discussion, and then I'll talk about my problems," I said as I tried to steer the conversation back to her.

"Sure, but there isn't that much more to tell," Anna said.

"How old is your neighbor?" I asked.

"I don't know, a little bit older than me. He's actually the son of the owners of the house. They seem to be away visiting family most of the time. I haven't seen them very often," said Anna.

"Maybe your young neighbor is in the drug business or something along that line. He really didn't need a barking dog to draw attention to whatever he was or is doing," I suggested.

"No, I don't think so. If he is dealing drugs, the buyers would be knocking at his door all hours of the day or night. That doesn't happen. He rarely, if ever, has company," Anna said.

"Okay, we'll keep working on that as a side line. We need an answer, don't we?" I asked Anna.

"We sure do," agreed Anna. "Now, what's with your problems on the home front?"

"Are you finished?" I asked Anna.

"Yeah, but don't change the subject. Spill it, Linds," coaxed Anna.

"Okay, okay, but let's pay up and get out of here. Don't forget to leave a tip. Working as a waitress is a hard job. I've done it, so I know," I told Anna, and I placed a couple of dollars on the table.

When we stepped outside the restaurant, I was surprised to see the dark clouds gathering over our heads.

"I didn't know it was supposed to rain," I mumbled.

"Neither did I," said Anna. "Let's hurry so we don't get wet."

I had avoided spilling my guts to Anna this time. I didn't think I was ready to hear myself speak out loud about my problems.

Chapter 10

Jed was waiting for me at my house when I arrived home after work.

I raced into the house to get dinner started, but much to my surprise, the food was ready and waiting for me. Jed had stopped at the local pizza shop and picked up pizza and pasta.

"Jed, did you do this?" I asked as I stood in the kitchen with my mouth open, which made me look totally stupid.

"Yep. I thought you could use a little break from cooking for everyone, including me, especially since I invited myself to your house," he answered with a grin.

"You know, you didn't have to do this," I muttered in appreciation.

"I know," he said shyly.

I looked at him and realized that I truly liked him and appreciated the fact that he was my friend.

"Emily, Ellen, get the plates and utensils down from the cabinets and set the table so we can eat. Ryan, get some napkins and sodas for all of us," I said as I ordered my happy children into action. Again, they were being treated to food that had already been prepared. It was so good to see them laugh and be happy.

"Let's eat!" shouted Jed.

The food was devoured in no time at all, and my content children departed to each of their bedrooms to do homework.

"Lindsay, would you like to go for a drive? We can go to the park to talk. You can tell me all about the robbery," he said in a pleading tone.

"Yes, okay. Just let me tell my kids where I will be," I said as I walked down the hall, knocking on doors.

Jed drove, and I enjoyed the pleasure of being a passenger. We located a picnic table, and we sat across from each other.

"Tell me about the robbery," Jed said softly.

"I had gone grocery shopping and as I was strolling through the store I heard a pop. Then I heard another pop, so I went to check it out. That's when I saw one of the robbers standing over the body on the floor. He was holding a gun and was looking around to see if anyone else was moving. I'm sure he would have shot them if he had seen any kind of movement," I said, crossing my arms in front of me rubbing on my arms as if I were cold.

"Are you cold?" Jed asked.

"No, not really. I just got a chill thinking about it, that's all," I answered as I tried to control my voice. I was on the verge of tears, and I really couldn't explain why.

"What happened next?" asked Jed.

"When that robber, the shooter, went into the manager's office, the other two were cleaning out the cash registers. I crawled up on the floor to blend in with the others who were all sprawled out and afraid to move. I tried to get a better look at the robbers, but all I could see were their eyes, especially the eyes of the shooter. I know I have seen those eyes before, and I know I will recognize them if I ever see them again, mask or no mask."

"Why?" he asked.

"They were just familiar, blue eyes. Then robbers all ran out to the parking lot, but before they went out the door, I think I heard a cell phone ring. I don't know if it belonged to someone lying on the floor or one of the robbers, but it was a distinctive, tinkling ring," I said as I concentrated on the ring, trying to not forget the sound. "I've never heard that ring again."

"You could have gotten yourself killed by trying to snoop around to see the robbers," scolded Jed.

"Yes, I know, but when I initially started snooping, as you put it, I didn't know what was happening. It was a pop, followed by another pop. I didn't know someone had been shot," I said with a rush of tears gushing from my eyes.

"Aw, Linds, I didn't mean to upset you," Jed said. He walked over to me to embrace me with all of the comfort he could offer.

I cried and cried until there were no more tears left. Jed held me in his arms until they subsided. His arms felt so safe and comfortable. His shoulder was perfect for resting my head.

I raised my head, shaking it from side to side, trying to clear my mind as I pulled myself away from his embrace.

"I'm so sorry, Jed. I don't usually fall apart. Actually, I'm always the one who is in complete control," I said as I moved further away from him.

"No problem, Lindsay. Just proves to me that you're a human being," he said with a forced smile.

It was quiet and a bit awkward. That was when I heard it.

"What is that?" I asked.

"What?" asked Jed.

"That noise," I answered.

"What noise?" asked Jed.

"It's a tinkling sound, almost like a music box, but muffled. Don't you hear it?" I asked as I furrowed my brow, making an effort to concentrate on the sound.

"I don't hear anything except the normal sounds," said Jed.

"There it goes again. Don't you hear that?"

"No, I'm sorry. I don't hear a muffled tinkling sound. Compare it to something, and I'll try to hear it," said Jed.

"It's, it's—I can't explain it. You have to hear it," I said with exasperation.

"Do you hear it all of the time?" asked Jed.

"No, just every once in a while. Now—I hear it now," I whispered.

Jed turned his head a bit and then heard something that he couldn't identify.

"What is that?" asked Jed.

"You heard it, didn't you?" I asked.

"I heard something. I have no idea what it was. Can you figure it out?" he asked.

I didn't answer right away because I was concentrating so very hard trying to place the sound.

"It's a cell phone. It is one of those odd-sounding ring tones," I said. I tried to relax my facial features.

"Where is it? Is it your cell that is ringing?" asked Jed.

"No, my phone just has a ring. I don't like all of that noise. Do you?" I asked.

"Me neither. I like a ring. I've seen cell phones where a certain ring identifies the person calling. I think that's a bit much," he said.

"It's either in something or under it. Look around and see if you can spot it anywhere," I instructed.

"I don't hear it now," said Jed.

"Neither do I," I agreed.

"It's getting late. We need to get out of here," Jed said as he tried to usher me to the car.

"Just a couple more minutes. I want to see if it rings again," I said.

"I'll wait in the car," said Jed as he tried to hide his displeasure.

I closed my eyes and concentrated on listening.

"Lindsay, come on. It's getting dark," shouted Jed.

"Okay, okay, I'm coming," I replied as I slowly walked to the car.

"Get in," he said.

"Yes, okay, I don't want it to be too dark before getting home." I climbed into the car and sat quietly as he drove toward my house.

My mind was spinning. The sound was haunting me. I knew I had heard if before hearing it in the park.

"I've heard that ring. I know I have," I mumbled as I walked to my front door. I turned to watch Jed put his car in reverse to back out and go home alone.

As my thoughts wandered, I thought about how Jed and I weren't a couple; we were just friends who shared time together. Sharing time seemed to be happening a lot lately. I liked that.

At home, I climbed into bed hearing the ring tone in my head.

The next morning I had an idea. I searched for the ring tone settings on my phone and listened to each one of them. There was nothing on my cell phone similar to what I had heard.

Later that same day, I asked Jed to do a search on his phone. He found nothing. No similar sound was found.

"Well, Jed, we know it isn't on our cell phones. Do you know anyone with a different service?" I asked. I wanted to pursue the elusive sound.

"No, but I'll ask around if you will do the same," he said.

Jed and I met for dinner a few days later to discuss my role as witness-victim. He was planning a human interest story on how a crime committed by one person can affect others.

We finished dinner. I was ready to go home. I headed to my car and as I climbed into my car to go home, I heard it again. The sound was coming from outside the car—from the driver side of the car. It had to be inside someone's parked car or in the pocket of someone who was standing near my car.

I looked up into the eyes of a man who was looking at me. I quickly ducked my head and started my car.

He jumped into an SUV and started his vehicle.

I glanced at where his license plate should be. It was covered with mud.

The only dirty spot on that vehicle was the license plate. How convenient.

Throwing my car into gear, I raced out of the parking lot and into what little traffic there was in the area.

Reaching for my cell phone I pressed Jed's number.

"He's following me!" I shouted into the speaker of my phone.

"Who?" asked Jed.

"The person, a man—the one with the ring tone. He saw me look up when I heard it go off," I said loudly.

"Where are you?" he demanded.

"On 460 headed home," I said as loudly as I could.

"Can you see him?" screamed Jed.

"Yes, he's right behind me. I think he is going to try to run me off the road," I said excitedly.

"Be careful. I'm coming. I'll try to catch a cop's attention with my driving. I'm sure the cop will follow me to help you," he said breathlessly. He stepped on the gas pedal and his engine gave an enormous roar. "Don't hang up the phone, Lindsay. Leave the line open so I can hear you."

"Okay," I answered with concentration on watching the road and the traffic, that was beginning to thin out a bit.

I glanced in my rearview mirror. The man's black vehicle, bigger than life, was filling the small, rectangular piece of glass.

"Oh, God!" I screamed. "He's right behind me."

I floored the gas pedal of my mid-sized Chevy Cavalier and tried to get away from him.

"I'm hanging up, Jed, so I can take a picture of him from my rearview mirror," I shouted.

"No, no, don't hang up!" Jed screamed.

Too late, Jed was gone. I had heard his pleading voice trailing off before he disconnected.

Picking up my cell phone, I aimed it at my rearview mirror. Once again, I could see the mirror was filled with the specter of the big, black SUV. With one hand, I began shooting pictures, barely glancing at the screen as I snapped the camera. As an afterthought I held my cell phone up and aimed it at the rear window.

"Sirens," I whispered as I glanced in my rearview mirror again. The black, SUV was moving back, farther away from me.

The sirens were getting closer.

I saw Jed's car racing toward me. The lights of the state-police car followed him.

I aimed my vehicle to the side of the road.

Jed slowed his car and followed me.

The state policeman positioned his vehicle to block both Jed and me from movement.

The state-police officer approached Jed's car with his gun drawn and then walked to my vehicle. I climbed out of my car with my hands raised, just as Jed was told to do.

"What do you two think you are doing?" asked the officer.

"He was trying to run me off of the road," I said excitedly.

"I was trying to attract your attention so we could help her," added Jed.

The officer looked at me and asked, "Who was trying to run you off the road?"

"I don't know who he was, but he was trying to kill me! I'm sure of it!" I excitedly answered.

"How did you get involved?" the officer demanded of Jed.

"She called me on my cell phone and told me she was in trouble," Jed explained.

"Why was he chasing you?" asked the officer.

"I heard his cell phone ring tone," I said softly.

"You what?" asked the officer.

"I heard his cell phone, and I knew he had been in the grocery store a few days ago," I said.

"So?" demanded the officer.

"I don't know 'so,' officer. I just know he was trying to run me off the road and maybe even kill me," I answered angrily.

The state police officer went through the normal procedures for traffic violations. It included speeding and evasion, followed by instructions that we each should drive our cars to the state police detachment for further investigation.

I was scared of what was ahead of me even though I was under the watchful eye of the state police.

Jed was worried about a speeding ticket and what it would do to his insurance rates.

We both were agreeable. We understood all of the regulations and rules that had been explained to us. All we wanted in return was for someone to listen to us and help us discourage any further harassment from the occupant of the black SUV.

I had to let my children know where I would be. When I entered my car to follow the officer to the police station, I quickly dialed my home telephone number. "Emily, I will be a little late getting home. You guys should finish your homework, if you haven't already done so, and get ready for bed," I explained hurriedly.

"Where are you?" asked Emily.

"I'm at the police station. Jed and I witnessed an incident, and we have to make a statement. I don't think it will take very long. But I will be getting home later than I had hoped. Love you all. If you need me, I have my cell phone," I said and quickly disconnected under the hard stare of the officer.

I didn't want to tell them that I was the one involved in the incident. They were already worried way too much for kids.

The interrogation continued at the state police detachment.

"Who were you driving away from?" asked an officer who appeared to be the man in charge of the place.

"I don't know," I answered. I had been separated from Jed for the follow-up interrogation.

"How do you know he was after you? Maybe he was just an aggressive driver?" continued the officer.

"He was on my bumper. I actually felt him bump me a couple of times. There is probably damage on my rear bumper," I explained.

The officer stood up and walked to the door, directing his voice to someone outside of the room.

"Go check the rear bumper of the lady's car," he said.

He stood next to the door until the answer was given to him.

"Yes, sir. There is damage to the rear bumper. Quite a bit of damage was done, and you can tell it happened recently," said an officer outside of the room.

"Okay, why was he after you?" asked the officer, who had returned to sit at the table to face me.

"I don't know why. I heard the ring tone of his cell phone when I was at the grocery store a few days ago. Jed was with me, and we really didn't know what the noise was at first. It took us a while to figure out the sound. The man with the ring tone saw me and remembered that I had heard it, the ring tone I mean, and that's when he came after me," I said.

"Why was that ring tone so important?" asked the officer.

"I don't know. I just don't know. Unless he was one of the robbers at the grocery store, and he knew that I knew he was there," I answered.

"You wait here for a while. I need to check with the local police department to see if they have arrested any suspects in the grocery-store robbery," said the officer.

"You need to wait in the area outside this room while I talk to your friend," the officer said when he returned to the small room. He ushered me into the waiting area where Jed was sitting.

"Ma'am, you have a seat," he instructed and motioned for Jed to follow him into the room I had exited. The door was open and I could hear every word of the conversation.

"Why were you speeding?" asked the officer as he looked directly at Jed.

"Lindsay needed help and that was the fastest way for me to help her," Jed answered.

"How do you know she needed help?" the officer demanded.

"She called me on my cell phone and told me she was being followed. I tried to get her to leave the line open, but she disconnected so she could take a picture of the black SUV following her," Jed said.

The officer rose from his seat and went to the door.

"Get the lady's cell phone," he instructed.

With cell phone in hand, he started going through the many photos stored on the phone. Finally, he found what he was looking for after he had scanned each photo slowly and thoroughly.

"Print the photos off that show the inside rearview mirror of the car that belongs to the lady. Also, print the ones of the back window. Just print them onto typing paper for us to look at for right now," he instructed.

"Sir, you can return to the waiting room with your friend," the officer said to Jed.

"Thank you," said Jed as he stood.

"What's happening now?" I asked when Jed sat on the seat next to me.

"They're printing the photos you took on your cell phone. I guess you did the right thing, Lindsay, when you disconnected my call and started taking pictures," Jed said.

"Jed, I'm so sorry about getting you into this whole mess," I said as I fought the deluge of tears building behind my eyes.

"What else could you do, Linds? He might have killed you," said Jed as he tried to console me.

We sat in the waiting room for hours. The officer who had questioned both of us directed us to follow him back into the small interrogation room.

"Have a seat," he said. "I'll tell you what I have discovered."

The officer placed a photo on the table in front of Jed and me. "Do you know this man?" asked the officer.

"No, sir," replied Jed.

"I recognize his face. He was the man chasing me. I don't know who he is or why he was after me," I said.

"We will be investigating this further, but for now, that is all we need from you two," said the officer.

"What about us?" I asked.

"Due to the circumstances of possible impending death, the Commonwealth Attorney said there will be no charges filed against either of you at this time," said the officer.

"Thank you, Officer," said Jed. "Before we leave, can you tell me if you know the other two people who were involved in the robbery?" asked Jed.

"That hasn't been determined yet," answered the officer.

"Are we out of danger?" I asked.

"I really can't answer that. We haven't yet located the man in the photo."

Jed and I walked out of the police station with stunned looks plastered to our faces.

We said good night to each other and departed in our separate cars. I was so grateful to have survived the evening.

Chapter 11

Home was so sweet. It was good to see my front door and all of the lights blazing in the house. All three of my sleepy-eyed children were sitting in the living room awaiting my arrival.

"Mom, what happened?" asked Ellen, racing toward me and then hugging me so very close.

"You need to go to bed. Tomorrow is a school day, so scoot. I'll tell you about everything that happened after school. I love you, and I want a kiss good night, please. I don't normally ask you to do that, but tonight I need a kiss from each of you now," I said, straining to keep from bursting into tears.

"Tell us now, Mom," begged Emily.

"No. No. Tomorrow. Now, please go to bed," I said in response, again struggling with my emotions.

One by one, each of my children hugged my neck, kissed my cheek, and shuffled off to bed.

I was about to fall asleep when my phone startled me back to wakefulness.

"Hello," I sputtered into the phone.

"Lindsay, did you get arrested this evening?" demanded a hateful voice.

"Who is this? Is that you, Justin?" I said in a sleep-filled voice.

"Yeah! I saw you at the police station in the middle of the night. What did you do?" Justin demanded.

"I didn't do anything, Justin. Now, please leave us alone and quit following me. Get a life, will you?" I said loudly and slammed the phone down to its cradle.

I realized that it was the middle of the night and that my loud voice and angry slamming of the telephone might have disturbed my children. I crawled out of my bed and walked up and down the hall to check for sounds from my kids.

Emily's and Ellen's rooms were quiet—no movement sounds. Ryan's room was silent at first, but after I stood outside an extra moment or two, I heard a muffled voice. I put my ear against his door.

"No, she didn't say," whispered Ryan.

There was a pause for conversation from the other end of the line.

"I'll call you tomorrow, after..." said Ryan.

I pushed open his bedroom door and startled Ryan as he hung up the telephone receiver.

"Who were you talking to?" I demanded in a stern whisper.

"No one. I called to check the time. I forgot to wind my alarm clock yesterday," he said calmly.

"Ryan, stop lying to me. I heard you talking to someone," I continued sternly.

"What were you doing snooping outside my door, Mom? Don't you trust me anymore?" he asked me.

"I know there is something or someone bothering you, Ryan. I can't help you unless you tell me about it. I love you, Ryan. Please tell me—what's wrong?" I pleaded with my young son.

"Nothing's wrong, Mom. Can I go back to sleep?" he asked sweetly.

"We will talk again tomorrow," I said as I closed his bedroom door.

I wandered back to my bedroom with all of Ryan's strange actions flashing through my mind. I had not punished him yet for any of the lies, but I knew the time was coming when I would have to take some kind of action. For the life of me, I didn't know what I should do. *Was Ryan being harassed by his father without my knowledge? Who was that Brian person he talked with on occasion? Why all of the lies?*

I slept fitfully that night. I moved around in a zombie-like state as I tried to get my kids ready for school. They were just as tired as I was, but they dressed, ate cereal, and walked outside to wait for the school bus. I was almost glad to be going to work so I could have something else to distract my mind for a few hours.

Chapter 12

I was in search of some kind of normalcy when I arrived at Wayne Maxwell's Law Office. Even though a law office could be a whirlpool of problems for everyone, client or employee, I knew those problems would be dealt with by using a step-by-step protocol as required by the legal system.

"Lindsay, line 1," said the cheerful voice of Anna over the intercom as I worked away at preparing the paperwork for a real-estate closing scheduled for the following week.

"Ms. Harris, this is Stacy Nelson from the Commonwealth Attorney's Office," said a female professional voice.

"Yes, Ms. Nelson, what can I do for you?" I answered as I sat up straight and focused my attention solely on the voice inside my phone.

"We need to schedule a time with you to go over your written statement about the incident that happened on September 20th at the Save-Mart in Stillwell, Virginia," she said, as if reading it from a script.

"Okay, but I want you to know that my employer, Wayne Maxwell, wants to come with me," I answered just as professionally.

"That's fine, Ms. Harris. Would tomorrow at 3 pm be good for the both of you?"

"Let me get his calendar. One moment, please," I said as I placed the call on hold.

Wayne was in his office, so I knocked gently and asked, "The Commonwealth Attorney's Office wants me to go over my written statement tomorrow at 3 pm. Is that good with you?" He glanced at his calendar and nodded his head in affirmation.

I returned to my office, where I removed the call from hold.

"Yes, tomorrow at 3 pm is fine for both of us," I said into the receiver.

"Good. Thank you, Ms. Harris. I will see you tomorrow," Stacy said softly before disconnecting the line.

That phone call threw a monkey-wrench into my desire for normalcy.

Wayne left the office to do a title search at the court house. I returned to preparing paperwork. Occasionally, my mind strayed to what I would say when I was asked about my statement. All I could do was tell the truth about what I had seen.

Wayne returned a couple of hours later with a revelation that completely derailed my day.

"Lindsay, two of the three robbers have been arrested," he said excitedly. "Do you think you will be able to recognize either of them?"

I looked at him as if he had lost his mind.

"Wayne, they wore masks," I sputtered.

"I know, I know, but you might recognize something about them. Just give it a try," he said as he urged me to comply.

"Sure, okay, Wayne. When?"

"Now. Right now. I'll go with you," he said as he tried to hurry me into leaving.

I stood behind the two-way glass and stared at the group of men. All had their faces covered with ski masks.

I remembered their eyes. So, I had no problems identifying the frightened eyes of two of the men, but the blue, penetrating eyes of the third robber were not there.

I understood clearly why I was being chased by the SUV. The driver was out to eliminate me. I was a witness, and he thought I could identify him. But for the life of me, I couldn't figure out who he was.

When I left the police station, I told Wayne I would meet him at the office as soon as I grabbed something to eat. I needed some alone time to think. I didn't want him hovering over me and trying to give me guidance for the time being.

Instead, I called Jed.

"Hi, Lindsay. What's happening?" he asked with concern.

"A lot," I said with a sigh. "I have to make a statement tomorrow at the Commonwealth Attorney's Office. But, the worst of it happened just a few minutes ago."

"What? What happened?" he asked.

"I had to go identify two of the robbers," I answered.

"How could you do that? Didn't you say they wore masks?" he asked.

"Yes, but it was their eyes. I recognized their eyes. They were as frightened today as they were during the robbery. It was almost too easy," I explained.

"Yeah, I guess. What about the third guy?" he continued.

"He was the shooter, and he wasn't in the line-up. I would bet my last cent on the fact that he was the one who tried to run me off the road and kill me," I said as calmly as I could.

"Yeah, you're probably right," he agreed. "I'll be at your house waiting for you when you get off work."

"No, no. Don't do that. I don't want you involved in any more of this," I said.

"I am involved, Lindsay," he said sternly but kindly.

Chapter 13

Jed was waiting for me along with two of my three children. I didn't realize anyone was missing at first glance, because everyone who was at home had scattered to their rooms to do homework or talk on the telephone, which was usually the case with Ellen and Emily.

I had prepared a meatloaf earlier in the day, mixing all of the ingredients so that it would be ready to pop into the oven as soon as I arrived home from work. It eliminated a lot of the delay time that came with getting the evening meal cooked and served.

"Ellen, go get your brother," I said as I mashed the potatoes.

"He's not here," she replied.

Without any real concern, I asked, "Where did he go?"

"I don't know. He didn't come home from school," she added.

"He what? Why didn't you tell me?" I asked harshly.

"I thought Emily told you. You know you sometimes let him go to his friend's house, so I thought that was what he did," Ellen explained.

"You both should have told me," I stormed at her. "Emily, get in here right now! Ellen, you finish mashing the potatoes and put everything on the table. Set a place for Jed, too," I instructed.

"What, Mom?" said Emily as she entered the kitchen.

"Where is your brother?" I asked.

"I don't know," she answered with a look of surprise.

"Why didn't you tell me he didn't come home from school?" I demanded.

"I didn't know I was supposed to do that. He told me you knew that he was going to Jason's house," she explained.

I looked for my address book that held Jason's mom's phone number and asked, "Did he go to Jason's house?"

"I guess so. I didn't pay attention to the stop when he got off the bus," she said apologetically.

I grabbed my address book and nervously started punching in the number on my phone.

"Hello," answered a soft voice.

Trying not to announce my anger, I said, "Mrs. Marston, this is Lindsay Harris. I'm Ryan's mom. May I speak with Ryan?"

"I'm sorry, Ms. Harris, but Ryan is not here. I haven't seen him. Are you sure he was supposed to come here?" she asked with interest.

"Well, that was what he told his sister. Is Jason there? May I speak with him?" I asked as I continued to track my son.

"Hello?" said a male voice that was deeper than Ryan's, but not by much.

"Jason, I'm Ryan's mom. Did he tell you where he was going after school?" I asked, as I again tried to control my voice, keeping it calm and less demanding.

There was a pause. Jason wasn't answering me.

"Jason, are you still there?" I asked.

"Yes, ma'am."

"Where did Ryan go after school?" I asked a bit more sternly.

"I can't tell you," he replied in a barely audible tone.

"Do you know where he went?" I said a little louder.

"Yes, ma'am."

"Then tell me, please," I said as I made myself speak softly.

"I can't," he answered.

"You can't or you won't? Which is it?"

"I can't."

"Why?" I demanded.

"I promised I wouldn't tell anyone," he said.

"I need to know where he is, Jason. Please tell me," I pleaded.

"I promised Ryan I wouldn't tell," he sputtered.

"Let me speak with your mom," I said.

I heard him telling his mother that I wanted to speak with her again.

"Mrs. Marston, your son knows where my son, Ryan, went after school. Please make him tell me. I don't know where Ryan is, and I have to find him. Please help me," I begged.

"Just a minute," said Mrs. Marston.

I heard the exchange of voices through the telephone, but I couldn't understand what mother or son was saying. There seemed to be a struggle over the telephone receiver.

"Tell her now," said a strong, harsh, female voice.

"He went to meet Brian," said Jason tearfully.

"Who is Brian? What is Brian's last name? Where did he go to meet him?" I asked in a barrage of questions.

"He got off in front of my house and climbed into a car. I don't know where they were going, and I don't know Brian's last name," he said between sobs.

"What kind of car was it?" I demanded.

"I don't know."

"What did Brian look like?" I continued.

"He was old," said Jason.

"How old? Like your dad?" I asked.

"Yeah, I think so," said Jason.

"What color was his hair?" I asked.

"Brown, and he wore dark glasses," said Jason.

49

I paused as I compared the description Jason gave me to the attributes of Justin, Ryan's father. It didn't appear to be him from the description. Of course, that was where my mind went when I lost track of Ryan. I was afraid his father had taken him.

Now, I didn't know which was the lesser of two evils.

Yes, I did. I knew I would have been able to live with the fact that his father had him. But that wasn't the case.

I didn't know who had Ryan or what he planned to do with my son.

"Jason, thank you for telling me. I'll let Ryan know that you tried to keep his secret," I told the tearful boy.

I hung up the receiver and went in search of Jed and my girls, all of whom sitting in the living room waiting for me to finish my phone call to Jason. "Emily, do you know Brian?" I asked.

"Brian who?" Emily asked me.

"How about you, Ellen? Do you know Brian?" I asked.

"No. Should I?" Ellen asked.

"No, not really. I was just hoping, I guess," I said as I turned to Jed.

"Tell me what to do, Jed. I just can't think any more. I was afraid his father had taken him again. But no, I think I was wrong. I don't know anyone named Brian," I said with the tears of anger and frustration erupting.

"Call 9-1-1," said Jed.

Chapter 14

"Ms. Harris, when did you last see your son?" asked the town police officer who was standing in front of me in my living room. He had such a large, imposing figure that he overwhelmed the small room and everyone in it.

"This morning before he went to school," I answered.

"What was he wearing?" asked the officer.

"Blue jeans and a green Stillwell Middle School T-shirt."

"Who was the last person to see him?" asked the officer.

"His friend Jason. Ryan had told his sister that I said it was okay for him to go to Jason's house. But he didn't," I answered and fought to keep the tears out of my voice.

"Where is this Jason?" continued the officer.

"He lives on the next street over. I already called, and Jason told me Ryan got into the car with a man named Brian," I explained.

"Who is Brian?" he asked.

"I don't know," I said as the sobs erupted again. "I only found out that he existed a couple of days ago when he called Ryan."

"Do you have a recent picture of your son?" asked the officer.

I turned to grab a photograph off the end table. "This is Ryan," I said and handed the framed 8 x 10 photograph to the officer.

"I'll get this out on the radio and issue an Amber Alert," the officer said as he handed the photograph to another officer standing next to him. "What about Ryan's father?" asked the officer.

"At first, I thought it was him, Justin, I mean, who took Ryan. After I talked with Jason, I realized it wasn't Justin. I'll give you his phone number. I don't know his address," I said. I wrote Justin's phone number down on a piece of paper that I handed to the officer.

"What should I do, Officer?"

"Nothing, ma'am. You should stay here and wait for a phone call from your son or the person who has him. We will put a trace on the line, so you will probably need to keep your conversations short unless the man calls to tell you why he took Ryan. Do you understand what I'm trying to say, Ms. Harris?" asked the officer.

"You want me to keep the child-snatcher on the line as long as possible but to be short with everyone else," I said in a sing-song tone.

"Yes, ma'am," said the officer in response.

"I don't have any money, Officer. I'm sure he is not after the money," I said in a much nicer tone. My sarcasm was trying to escape again.

"Where do you work, ma'am?" he asked.

"For Wayne Maxwell, a local attorney. As far as I'm aware, he isn't into any really scary cases," I explained.

"What about you, ma'am?" he probed.

"What about me? I'm a legal secretary–assistant, and I work for Wayne—Oh, oh, oh! Maybe it's about the grocery store robbery," I said as I blanched to a sickly white.

"You mean the Save-Mart?" asked the officer.

My mind was spinning. What had I done?

"Yes, sir," I finally answered.

"How are you involved?" continued the officer.

"I was there during the robbery. I was on the floor with the other customers," I explained.

"Did you know the perpetrators? The robbers?" he asked.

"No, they wore masks. Just today at the police station, I was able to identify two of the three men involved. I recognized their eyes," I said as I shook my head from side to side. "It was probably a mistake to do that, wasn't it?"

"No, ma'am. It's your duty to help in an investigation any way that you can by providing all the information that you have," he said as he tried to soothe me.

"Maybe it's the third guy. He's the one they haven't arrested yet. Maybe he took my son," I said as I realized the possibility.

Jed jumped up from his seat on the easy chair and threw his arms around me.

"Don't worry, Lindsay, they'll catch him and find Ryan. You know they will," he said as he tried to hold me together emotionally.

I wanted to cry, to scream, to punch someone. Jed was holding me tight. He didn't want me to break loose and start swinging.

The officer left the room. I was thinking that he went to question Jason.

Jed, Emily, Ellen, and I sat in the living room, stunned but restless.

"Mom, I'm so sorry I didn't tell you earlier," said Ellen.

"Don't worry about that, girls. That's all over and done with. We just need to concentrate on getting Ryan back."

"How?" asked Emily.

"We'll help the police any way we can. I'm going to go check Ryan's room to see if I can find anything at all related to Brian. Maybe the police officers overlooked something," I said. I stood up and moved from the sofa just to fulfill the need to move, to help, to do something.

Chapter 15

Jed helped me search through Ryan's private things, looking for any mention of Brian. We found nothing—no phone numbers, no scribbling referring to Brian, no mention whatsoever of the man who had kidnapped my son.

It was getting late into the night, and I was exhausted. My girls had dropped off to sleep in the living room chairs.

"Em, El, you need to go to your rooms so you can rest better," I told my girls in a whisper. I didn't want to frighten them by using a loud, demanding voice.

They had a hard time focusing their sleep-filled eyes, but then they returned to reality, stood, and stumbled to their rooms. Even though they were twins, I had let each girl have her own bedroom to live in and do whatever. Oddly enough, their tastes, just like their personalities, ran along the same lines. But they did like their own private moments in their separate rooms.

I found Jed dozing in the living room after he had helped me search Ryan's room.

"Jed, you need to go home and get some rest. I'll call you if anything happens around here," I said. I watched him wake up enough to understand what I was saying.

"Are you and the girls going to be okay?" he asked.

"Yes, I think so. A town policeman will be present for at least a few more hours. They will be waiting for a phone call. You go on home and go to work tomorrow. I'll give you a call when anything happens. I promise. Okay?" I said as I encouraged him to get into his bed for a couple hours of sleep.

Sleep for me was not going to happen. I knew I had to call Ryan's father to tell him what was happening before he heard it on the news or read it in the newspaper. I punched in the numbers to reach Justin.

"Hello," he said angrily. I looked at the clock on the end table and realized it was 2 am.

"Justin, it's Lindsay," I said softly.

"What's wrong? Why are you calling me at this time of night?" he grouched at me.

"It's Ryan. He has been kidnapped," I said. I fought hard to control the flood water that was building up behind my eyes.

"How? Why? When?" he sputtered venomously.

"It's a long story. I'll tell you what I know," I said with a sigh.

I told him everything and, of course, he blamed me for Ryan's disappearance.

"It would not have happened if I'd had him!" he screamed at me.

"Maybe so," I answered loudly. "But I didn't expect the grocery store to be robbed when I went shopping. How could I have known that was going to happen? I needed you to tell me that, Justin," I snapped sarcastically. I fought the angry tears that were threatening to overwhelm me.

"I'll be over there shortly!" he yelled.

"No, don't come here. The police will be visiting you, so you just stay put. They will give you a call to check you out just to make sure that you aren't behind this kidnapping!" I screamed back at him.

"I didn't take, Ryan," he blustered.

"I know. That's what I told them. But they will check you out anyway. Just do as they say. Please, Justin," I pleaded in a calmer tone.

I hung up the phone and began crying. This time, the tears were bitter tears of anger and frustration. I just could not hold them inside any longer. Why couldn't Justin and I communicate in normal tones without having it become screaming competition? This was something I couldn't understand.

Chapter 16

I collapsed onto the sofa. I couldn't bring myself to stand up, look alert, or be strong one more second. But as exhausted as I was, my mind was racing. My brain was projecting one bad scenario after another, showing me in vivid, living color what could happen to my son. I didn't want to go to bed. I needed to be awake in case the phone rang. I forced myself back up from the sofa. I had to move around to keep my body awake and force my mind to stop playing the bad scenarios over and over again.

I walked into the kitchen, where I spotted two men sitting at the table drinking coffee. The two officers were waiting for a phone call so they could trace it.

"Why haven't they called?" I asked in a hoarse whisper.

"I don't know, ma'am. I thought they would have contacted you by now," said a sleepy-eyed officer.

"I did, too," I agreed.

"You probably need to go to bed and get some sleep, ma'am. I doubt that we will get a call until morning," said the officer.

"Yes, you're probably right," I mumbled as I turned to leave the kitchen. I stopped long enough in the living room to glance around at the disarray. I shook my head from side to side as I thought of the clean-up work ahead of me. I stumbled on toward my bedroom, where I fell onto my bed, my eyes closing before my head hit the pillow.

That was when the nightmares started. One image after another raced in my mind with my son beaten and tortured until he died. I knew it was only a dream even while I was dreaming because the images were surrounded by a hazy, cloud-like frame.

Suddenly, the phone began to ring. There was no phone in the nightmare. It had to be real. I forced myself to open my eyes. It was real. The phone was ringing.

I jumped from my bed and rushed to the kitchen where the police officers were waiting for me to answer it. "Hello?" I said breathlessly into the mouthpiece.

Dead silence.

"Hello, hello!" I screamed.

Silence.

"Who are you? Where is my son?" I begged angrily.

Dial tone.

I pulled the phone away from my face and held it in front of me. I wanted to throw it and make it shatter against the wall.

One of the officers grabbed it from my hand just as I started to lift my arm to give some momentum to the throw.

"Give it to me, ma'am," said the officer, and he struggled to take the phone receiver from me.

I looked at him in surprise and realized what I was about to do.

"Why did he hang up?" I sputtered between angry sobs.

"Just testing you. He wanted to see who would pick up the phone," explained the officer. He had been quiet both times that I had been in the kitchen.

"Well, I guess he knows now that I'm here and waiting for instructions. I hope he doesn't hurt Ryan," I cried.

The officers nodded and continued waiting vigilantly as I returned to my bedroom with no hope of going back to sleep.

I lay on my bed, on my back, with my eyes wide open. I was afraid to close them.

I heard my girls beginning to stir around in their rooms. I took a quick shower, put on fresh jeans and a T-shirt. I went to the kitchen to make a fresh pot of coffee. I had left the coffee ingredients and supplies out of the cabinet so the officers could make more for themselves if they wanted.

It looked like they had done just that, and they were brewing a fresh pot as I walked into the kitchen. The girls came into the kitchen wearing their pajamas.

"I'm making bacon, eggs, and toast for breakfast, girls. Do you think you will be able to go to school today?" I asked.

"No, we want to wait for Ryan," said Ellen.

"That's right," chimed Emily.

"Okay, but go take your showers and put on some fresh clothes. Believe me, a shower will help you feel a little better," I instructed.

"Have you heard anything yet, Mom?" asked Ellen.

"No, honey," I answered.

"Did I hear the telephone ring during the night?' asked Emily.

"Yes, but when I answered it no one was on the other end. Must have been a wrong number," I said, trying to gloss it over so it wouldn't appear as important as I had thought it was.

The girls left the kitchen, and I started frying bacon. We usually only had a big breakfast on the weekends, but I needed to keep myself busy. I had to be busy. I had to be doing something or I would surely go crazy.

The bacon grease was draining from the bacon after I finished frying it, and I was getting bread from its wrapper when the phone rang. I was startled by the loud ring, and I turned toward the kitchen table where the two officers had been stationed during the night. They had left the kitchen to allow me to cook. Upon hearing the loud ring, they ran back into the kitchen, grabbing their equipment and motioning for me to pick up the telephone when they signaled. I took a deep breath and waited. On the fifth ring, I picked up the receiver.

"Hello?" I said with an expelled breath.

"Lindsay?" said Justin.

"Yes, what do you want, Justin?" I asked with absolutely no air of kindness.

"Have the police found Ryan?" he asked softly.

"NO! No. You need to hang up because the kidnapper might call," I explained in a rush of words.

"Call me when you hear something," said Justin.

"I will, Justin. I promise," I said as I disconnected the line.

Again, I wanted to cry. I wouldn't allow myself to do so. The girls were returning to the kitchen, and I knew I had to be strong for them.

"Who was on the phone?" asked Ellen.

"Your father checking to see if I had any new information," I said softly.

"Oh," said Ellen.

"How do you want your eggs, Ellen?" I asked through a fake smile.

"Scrambled," she replied.

"Me, too," added Emily.

I finished up the breakfast dishes and sat down at the kitchen table with a fresh hot cup of coffee. The two officers were once again stationed in the kitchen, waiting for a phone call.

Ring-g-g-g.

I knew there would be a phone call, but my nerves were so on edge that every new ring startled me.

At the officers' signal, I picked up the receiver.

"Lindsay?"

"Yes, I'm Lindsay. Who is this?" I asked sternly.

"I am the person who has your son," said the soft-spoken voice.

"Why?" I asked.

"I need your cooperation," he replied.

"For what?" I asked.

"The robbery," he answered.

"What about the robbery?" I asked as I tried to keep him talking.

"I don't want you to identify me. I don't want you to do that!" he said angrily.

"How can I? You wore a mask," I said.

"You identified my partners by their eyes. I don't want that happening to me," he snarled.

"It won't. I promise. That that will not happen," I answered with my voice getting louder with each response.

The line was silent.

"Hello, are you there?" I screamed into the mouthpiece.

One of the officers grabbed for the phone again, pulling it out of my shaking hands.

"Let me have it, ma'am," coaxed the officer.

"Did you get it? Did you get his phone number?" I asked excitedly.

"It's an untraceable cell phone," he answered.

"Now what?" I asked.

"Now we wait. The department will continue to investigate and try to track down the third robber. When we find him, we will find your son," assured the officer.

"Wait, wait, wait." I mumbled as I left the kitchen in search of something, anything, to do.

Chapter 17

I had started straightening the living room when I remembered that I needed to call Jed. I told the officers I was making a personal call, hoping that they wouldn't record it.

"Jed, this is Lindsay," I said quietly.

"Hi, is he home?" he asked excitedly.

"No," I answered as I tried to control my voice and tried to hold back the tears.

"What's happening?" he asked.

"Waiting. That's all. I'm so tired of waiting," I said. My tears surfaced again. I took a deep breath and forced my tears back.

"I'm sure the police are doing everything they can. I'm going to jump in the car and come over and keep you company," Jed said. It was his way to pull me up from the depths of despair.

"You don't have to do that," I said in a tone that lacked sincerity.

"Yes, I do. How are the girls doing?" he asked.

"They are okay. They didn't go to school today and that was fine with me. It has been a comfort to have them around so I know exactly where they are," I explained.

"I'm going to go jump in my car right now. I'll be there soon, Lindsay," he said and hung up the phone. He did not give me a chance to say no.

I paced the floor. Waiting—waiting for a call.

The girls were in and out of their rooms, periodically, checking for news.

I was trying to figure out who had my son. From the way that he talked to me on the telephone, I must know him.

Why would I know him? Why would I recognize him? I didn't recognize the other two robbers until they had been in police custody. I would not have been able to identify them if they hadn't been arrested. I actually had never met either of them. I had only seen their eyes at the robbery. *Why would the kidnapper think I would know him? Who could it possibly be?*

There was a knock at my door, and the two police officers came running from the kitchen.

"Move away from the door, ma'am," they ordered.

"It's Jed, my friend. He's not the one you're after!" I shouted. But it was too late. They drew their guns from leather holsters.

"Are you sure?" asked an officer as he took aim at the front door.

"Yes, I saw his car turn into my driveway," I explained.

One of the officers walked to the door with his gun drawn. He opened the door, allowing Jed to enter. The second officer continued to aim his gun at Jed.

"Whoa-a-a! Tell them who I am, Linds!" he pleaded as he held up his hands in submission.

"I did," I sputtered angrily. "They are just trying to make us safe and not sorry," I assured him with a normal talking voice. The officers holstered their guns and returned to the kitchen to wait for a phone call.

"You look so tired, Linds," Jeb said with compassion. He was looking straight at me.

"I am. I didn't get much sleep. I need to tell you about the phone calls," I whispered. "I need to tell you, but I don't want the police officers overhearing our conversation."

"Did the kidnapper call?" asked Jed.

"Yes, but there were two other calls as well," I whispered. "The first one called and hung up. The second one was from my ex-husband checking for news about Ryan. The third call was the robber! He admitted that he has Ryan. All he told me was that he didn't want me to identify him. Why he would tell me that? I don't have a clue. He wore a mask, and all I saw was his eyes. Why does he think I can identify him?"

"You identified the other two," Jed said.

"Yes, but they were in police custody. I wouldn't have been able to do that if they hadn't been arrested and put in a line-up," I explained.

"You didn't recognize anything about him?" asked Jed.

"Between you and me, Jed, his eyes looked familiar, like I had seen him somewhere before that day, but I can't remember where," I said softly.

"Then he does have a reason to believe you can identify him, doesn't he?" said Jed.

"I guess so," I replied.

"Well, now we wait," said Jed.

"Yes, we wait and wait."

We were interrupted with, "Mom, what are we having for lunch?" asked Emily as she entered the room.

"Soup and sandwiches," I replied.

"When?" continued Emily.

I looked at the clock hanging on the wall and said, "Now. I'll go fix everything right now."

"Jed, do you want to keep me company in the kitchen?" I asked as I stood.

"Won't it be too crowded with those two officers in there, too?" he asked.

"No. They will probably come into the living room to get out of the way," I replied. The officers did exactly that.

They were going to have soup and sandwiches with us, so I prepared two kinds of canned soups since I didn't have enough of one flavor to feed us all.

I decided to serve the officers first. I asked them to get what they wanted and to go ahead and take it into the living room to eat so they could relax a bit.

Then I gathered my girls, along with Jed, and we helped ourselves to what was left.

"Mom, what's taking so long to get Ryan back home?" asked Emily.

"I wish I knew," I replied.

"What do you want us to do, Mom?" asked Ellen.

"There is nothing you can do right now. Unless—do you have any idea who might have taken him?" I asked Ellen, who answered by shaking her head.

"Mom, I need to call some friends later to get some homework assignments," said Emily.

"I know. Just don't stay on the phone any longer than necessary. We are still waiting for the phone call," I said with a sigh.

"What if they don't bring him back?" asked Emily.

"That's not going to happen, Em. I won't let that happen," I said sternly.

"How are you going to stop it?" asked Ellen.

"I can't. But those police officers in the living room and all of their coworkers will do just that. You girls need to clean up your rooms and bring me your dirty clothes. We'll get pizza for dinner. You both like pizza, don't you?" I asked remembering how Emily stared at the pizza delivery boy.

"That's sounds good, Mom," said Emily as she blushed.

Chapter 18

The afternoon dragged on with no call. I was tired of waiting and doing nothing. I was sure the two officers stationed in my kitchen were tired.

Jed was with me, and I truly appreciated the company of my friend. He offered me a good shoulder to cry on and that was all I wanted. I had no time for any other kind of commitment.

Justin was still in my life, not as a husband or lover, but as a specter that appeared before me quite often when he professed he would be the father he should have been for fourteen years. He was a constant reminder of the bad choices that I had made, and I truly didn't want to repeat that mistake again.

The telephone rang, and I took off running from the living room to the kitchen.

After receiving the pick-it-up signal from the officers, I apprehensively answered, "Hello?"

"What is happening?" demanded Justin.

"We're waiting, Justin. That's all I can do right now," I said angrily.

"If I had the kids, this wouldn't be happening," he snarled.

"I agree with you on that," I said. My impatience and anger were growing by leaps and bounds. I didn't want to lose it. I wanted to remain calm, displaying some modicum of control.

"When the police find Ryan, are you going to let me take him fishing?" he asked with a little more kindness.

"What? No. You know that, Justin. Drop it, will you? I just want to think about getting my son back," I replied with constraint in my voice tone.

"Do you know who has him?" asked Justin.

"It's the third robber from the grocery-store robbery that happened a few days ago. I was one of the shoppers who became a victim by accident. The robber thinks I can identify him. I really can't because they wore masks. But the man, for some reason, thinks I know who he is," I explained even though I didn't want to tell him anything.

"It is your fault, isn't it?" he said with what sounded like glee in his voice.

"Well, I guess so, Justin. Maybe I shouldn't go grocery shopping anymore," I said and disconnected the line.

"Are you okay?" asked Jed.

"I'm not going to cry," I mumbled. "I'm not going to cry. I'm not going to let him push my buttons."

"Settle down, Linds. He knows he can get you rattled, and that's obviously something he likes to do."

"Yeah, I know."

"Do you want me to go get pizzas?" asked Jed.

"No. No, I'm going to have them delivered. Emily seems to have a crush on the pizza-delivery boy or, I should say, man. I'm not sure how old he is, but he has to be old enough to drive. That makes him at least sixteen. Nothing will come of it, I hope. I just don't need to completely discourage all friendships and crushes for my girls," I said. I knew this was entirely too much about nothing, but I needed to talk.

"Sure, no problem," Jed answered.

"I'm going to go make that call now," I said as I went to the kitchen to get the phone number.

"I'm going to order pizzas. Do you guys want me to get one for you?" I asked the two officers stationed at my kitchen table.

"Yes, ma'am, but we'll pay for ours if you want to go ahead and order it for us," said the officer closest to the phone.

Everyone told me what toppings they wanted, and I ordered three large pizzas. In no time at all, there was a knock at the door. I collected money from the officers and Jed, got my money, and ran to the front door. I peeked out the small window before reaching for the lock.

Those eyes were staring into the window, waiting for me to open the door. I glanced down and saw that he was holding three pizza boxes in his hands. I froze as I stared into his eyes again. I turned the doorknob and greeted him with a smile.

"Hi," I said with a big smile.

"That's $24.66, ma'am, for all three pizzas," he said with an apprehensive grin.

I handed him thirty dollars and said, "Keep the change. By the way, what's your name? I want to tell your boss what a nice young man you are."

"Brian White, ma'am. Thank you," he replied, and he stared intently into my eyes. There was a smirk on his face and not the humble smile I was expecting.

I closed the door and stood for a few moments as I tried to figure out what I should do.

He was testing me. He had to be, or he wouldn't have delivered pizzas to my home.

I hoped I hadn't shown signs of recognition. Usually my emotions were very readable on my face. My face is a blatant display of my true emotions, a quality I inherited from my grandmother, so I'm told.

I carried the pizzas to the kitchen and told everyone to help themselves. I didn't really feel like eating—at least, not after paying for the pizzas. I picked and probed the slice I had on my paper plate until everyone was finished.

I quickly pulled Jed aside and said, "It's the pizza-delivery boy. He has Ryan."

"What? Are you sure?" Jed excitedly questioned in a whisper.

"It's his eyes. I saw his eyes at the grocery store. I know it's him. I tried to hide my reaction from him. I don't think he knew I recognized him," I explained further.

"Aren't you going to tell the police?" Jed asked.

"I don't know. I don't want Ryan to be killed, and I'm absolutely sure that will happen if the police show up at the Pizza Place," I said.

"Maybe we should do something, just the two of us," Jed suggested.

"That's what I was thinking. I told Brian White—that's his name—that I was going to call his boss and commend him for such good service. I think I'll do that right now," I said. I walked toward the kitchen to let the officers know that I was going to make a personal phone call.

I returned to the living room where I picked up the extension and entered the Pizza Place telephone number again.

"Hello, may I speak with the manager?" I asked after I listened to the lengthy greeting from the young lady who had answered the ring.

She put me on hold, and I waited a few moments listening to the pre-recorded Pizza Place sales information.

"Hello, may I help you?" asked the business-like male voice.

"My name is Lindsay Harris, and I wanted to let you know that you have a wonderful young delivery man, Brian White, in your employment," I gushed.

"Why thank you, ma'am. We've had many nice remarks about Brian White. He is a little bit older than most of our delivery people, but most everyone seems to like him," said the manager.

"How much older is he?" I asked.

"He's in his late twenties. He said he wanted to learn the pizza business from the ground up and that is just what he is doing," answered the manager.

"How long has he been working for you?" I probed.

"A couple of months. Now, if you don't mind, I need to get back to work," the manager said in his attempt to end the conversation.

"One more question, please," I said.

"What is it you want to know?" he asked politely.

"I want to make sure I get him each time I call. What days and hours does Brian White work? I have a teenage daughter who has a crush on young Mr. White," I said with a forced laugh.

"Tuesday, Thursday, Friday, and Saturday from 4 to 10 pm. He's so dependable. I never have to worry about calling anyone else in to take his place. Actually, I have called on him to fill in for others who don't show up," the manager answered hurriedly.

"Thank you, sir. You'll be getting more pizza orders from me," I said as I hung up the phone.

"Well, what did he say?" asked Jed.

"He gets off work at 10 pm. We need to be sitting and waiting for Brian White when he goes home," I said, looking around hoping my voice hadn't carried to anyone other than Jed.

"What are you going to tell those two guys who are stationed in your kitchen?" asked Jed.

"I don't know yet," I answered truthfully.

Chapter 19

I told my girls to dress in dark clothes. I did the same. We all, Jed included, went out to the car at 8:30 pm, ostensibly for the 9 pm showing of a movie that the girls wanted to see. That was a bold-faced lie. I hadn't been able to think of anything else to tell the officers.

Once inside the locked car, I told my daughters what Jed and I were planning to do. Emily was so disappointed to discover that her heartthrob was a criminal. Also, she had no idea that he was so much older than she was.

"Girls, keep your eyes open. We don't want to miss him. Your brother's life may be at stake," I cautioned. "Remember, he is a bad person, and he probably has bad friends who are helping him."

It may not have been the smartest, most motherly move to bring my daughters along on a job such as the one we were attempting, but I didn't want to leave them at the house with two officers who weren't there to babysit. Deep in my heart, I knew they would want to be able to say that they had a hand in saving their brother.

"Mom, what are we going to do if we see him?" asked Ellen.

"Follow him. We need to find Ryan, and I think that is the way to do it," I answered.

The girls settled back and seemed to be excited about the fact that I had included them.

I turned onto the bank parking lot, which was located on a hill across the road from the Pizza Place. I couldn't park in the Pizza Place lot because it was almost empty of cars, and I wouldn't have been able to explain to anyone—including myself—that I had a legitimate reason to be there.

There was a car wash adjacent to the Pizza Place. The car wash was closed, so there were no vehicles on the grounds to provide a spot where I could park and hide.

The bird's-eye view from across the road was best. There was a little distance. I would have to be careful and keep my eye on his vehicle as I navigated my way back to the road.

The girls sat in the back of the car and talked to each other in excited whispers. It was almost like a fun family outing, except that Ryan wasn't with us. In his place, we had the company of Jed, for which I was grateful.

I was a strong woman, but my shoulders sometimes sagged from the burden of single-motherhood. It really felt good to have a little bit of support, even if it were only temporary.

From the car, Jed and I kept watch through the front windshield, with an occasional glance out of the rear window for good measure.

Emily and Ellen stared intently out of each side window, turning periodically to look out the back window and then glancing toward the front.

After about an hour of this constant watching, we were all feeling the strain.

"There. Is that him?" asked Jed as he pointed toward a man walking across the parking lot.

"It looks like him, but we're so far away, I can't be sure," I said with dismay.

"He's on foot. Was he using a company car for deliveries?" asked Jed.

"Looks that way, doesn't it? Where could he be walking to at this time of night? There are no buses, and I didn't see anyone parked and waiting for him," I answered.

The figure was walking toward the road.

"He is going to cross the road. If he does that, I won't be able to see him," Jed said and opened the car door to jump out and peer down the hillside.

"Stay here, girls," I commanded. I followed Jed and stood beside him while we watched the figure walk up the inclined road.

"I hope he doesn't see us," I whispered to Jed.

"Me, too," he replied.

We didn't want to get back into the car until he had completely passed us. We moved so that we could stand behind the car, where we wouldn't be so easily seen. Opening the car doors would have caused the interior lights to shine like a beacon.

He must have felt our presence because he kept looking around, searching for any kind of movement or activity. The girls were whispering so I shushed them by placing my index finger upright against my lips. They looked at me with wide eyes and immediately got quiet.

"Where do you think he is going?" I asked Jed.

"Maybe he parked his car up here. We will just have to keep watching him to find out where he's going step," said Jed.

He continued to walk up the incline, keeping a watchful eye on his surroundings. When he had finally passed us, we both climbed back into the car, starting it without turning on the headlights. We were dreading the fact that as soon as I put the car into drive, the bright lit headlights would automatically turn themselves on, which up until now, I thought was a great safety feature.

"Here goes," I said as I rammed the gear into drive and slowly gave the gas pedal of my old Chevy Cavalier a nudge to get it moving very slowly.

All I wanted to do was keep the young man in sight.

I drove out of the bank parking lot and into the mall parking lot where I faced, head-on, brightly lit store fronts and a well-lit parking lot.

We weren't out of place, as we cruised this parking lot. Even at this time of night, there were several vehicles parked or inhabited by people who were waiting for others to come out of the mall. After all, it was near closing time for most of the business establishments.

I pulled between two cars almost directly in front of the mall entrance, when I noticed my mistake.

"That's not Brian White, Jed," I said angrily.

"It's not?" he asked with surprise.

"No. We've been following the wrong man," I said with disappointment.

I put the gearshift on the 'D' and took off out of the mall parking lot as fast as I could without causing an accident. I pulled into the parking lot of the Pizza Place and was disappointed to find that it was closed up tight.

"I guess we missed him," I said. Once again, I fought back angry tears.

Chapter 20

We had been gone long enough for the lie that I had told the officers to seem true. We walked into the house sad and tired. I sent the girls on to bed.

"Jed, you need to go on home," I said as we both found a seat in the living room. "Obviously, there had been no phone call, or the officers would have mentioned it to me when we arrived home."

"I thought I would just stay here on your sofa," he said with a smile.

"No. Don't do that. I already have two strong police officers staying here. They seem to change shifts every twelve hours. There are always two men posted here in the house with me," I explained.

Jed seemed disappointed as he rose from his seat and walked to the door and opened it to let himself out. When he opened the front door, he spotted an envelope stuck to the lower part of the glass.

"Lindsay, there is an envelope taped to your front door," said Jed in a loud whisper.

I glanced behind me to see if my watchers, the officers, had heard him.

"Let me have it," I told Jed.

He pulled the sealed envelope from the door and handed it to me. I ripped it open and read:

DON'T SAY ANYTHING OR......................

A photo of Ryan that had been printed from a computer and onto white paper that fell to the floor.

Ryan was crying.

I burst into tears. It was more that I could bear.

Jed closed the front door, led me to the sofa, and sat next to me with his arms wrapped around me to comfort me.

I could not be comforted. I didn't want to be comforted. I wanted my son back home with me. I sat next to Jed on the sofa, crying myself to sleep. My sleep was tormented with nightmares. One scene I swirling rather than standing still, but I could clearly see what was happening. I could see bodies floating past my eyes. I wanted to reach out and grab hold of one to make the motion stop. I could see a blond-haired boy, and I knew that it was Ryan. I lunged at the floating figure, but my hand could not grasp the flailing arms floating before me.

"Ryan! Stop! Ryan!" I screamed.

"Lindsay, Lindsay, wake up," Jed whispered harshly as he shook me gently.

"What? Hunh?" I sputtered as my mind made the jump from dream to reality.

"Lindsay, are you okay?" Jed asked.

"I think so. It was just a bad dream. I was so close to catching Ryan. He was just out of my reach," I cried.

"It was a dream," said Jed softly.

"No, no, it was more than that. I believe Ryan is just out of my reach. But I also believe I'm going to get him back. I have to believe that. I know I'm going to get him back home," I said as my crying began to subside.

There was no more sleeping for me that night. I got up from the sofa, and after I had found a pillow and a blanket, I told Jed to stretch out and get comfortable.

I walked into the kitchen, grabbed a cup of coffee, and sat at the table with the officers.

At dawn, I was still talking with the officers about anything and everything.

The phone rang around 7 am. Again, I was startled into the here and now, and I reached to pick up the receiver. The officers cautioned me to keep him on the line as long as possible.

"Hello?" I said apprehensively.

"Lindsay?" said a strange voice.

"Who is this?" I asked.

"Your son is fine for now, but you know what you have to do," said the peculiar-sounding voice.

I knew he had to be disguising it some way. Maybe he was straining it through a towel. It certainly didn't sound like Brian White.

"Why are you doing this? Is Ryan okay? Can I speak to him?" I shouted into the phone.

"Mom, Mom, when can I come home?" asked a scared Ryan. His voice was so strained. I knew he was trying not to break down and cry.

"I love you, Ryan. Soon. We will get you back real soon," I said as I heard the line disconnect.

"Ms. Harris, did you recognize the voice?" asked one of the officers.

"No, how could I? He had disguised his voice. It sounded muffled. I couldn't tell if it was a man or a woman," I said with exasperation.

"Did you hear anything in that call that might indicate where the call originated?" asked the officer.

"No sir, I did not," I stammered in reply.

I thought about what I had just said. Did I hear something? I closed my eyes shutting out all things around me. *Think, think,* I told myself.

"Ms. Harris, are you sure you didn't recognize any background noise?" the officer probed.

I shook my head from side to side. I still had my eyes closed, trying to force my tired brain to focus on the memory of the phone call. There had been some background noise, but what? No way was I going to be able to figure that out by myself. The police were going to have to do it—if it could be done at all.

I was beginning to lose my faith in the local police. I believed the FBI should be investigating this, but I had been told it wouldn't happen since state lines hadn't been crossed. The police believed that Ryan was being held locally, and it was a local murder investigation that was underway.

I walked into the living room where I saw Jed sitting up on the sofa, wide awake, waiting for me to tell him who had been on the telephone.

"It was him, Jed. We really need to get Ryan back before this guy does something really, really stupid," I whispered conspiratorially.

"Yes, we do," he replied.

Chapter 21

The day dragged by minute after minute because Jed and I were waiting for nightfall and planning another nighttime excursion to find Brian White's hiding place. We were sure we would find Ryan by following Brian. No one could convince us otherwise.

"Mom, can we go, too?" asked Ellen. She whispered the question to me after lunch and after I had told the girls what we were planning to do.

"Yes, but you can't say anything about it in front of the officers. Promise me. Both of you, please promise me, okay?" I asked as I cautioned them.

This time, the excuse to leave the house was going to be to go to an all-night drugstore where I could pick up some emergency feminine products for the girls. I didn't think they would question that as an excuse.

We would all go for a chance to get out of the house for a few minutes and that would be the explanation why the four of us would be traipsing out to the car.

We left at 8:30 pm, just like the evening before, and we waited in the bank parking lot located across the road and on the hill.

This time we were not going to be fooled.

I handed my cell phone to Emily after entering the Pizza Place number and told her to ask for Brian White.

"May I speak with Brian White?" she asked in her young, teenage girl voice.

"He's out on a delivery. May I take a message?" asked the older male voice on the other end of the phone.

I shook my head from side to side so she wouldn't leave anything that could be written down on a piece of paper. Of course, I had totally forgotten that 'Lindsay Harris' would be boldly displayed on the caller ID.

"No, sir. No message," said Emily as she handed me the phone.

"What did he say?" I asked Emily.

"He is out on a delivery," she answered.

"Good, we can wait right here for him to return with the money, and he can put it in the cash register," I said with an anxious smile.

No sooner had I finished that statement than a car drove into the Pizza Place parking lot, brandishing a removable delivery sign positioned on the roof over the top of the driver's side of a car.

"That's him," I whispered. I saw a young man climb out of the car.

The girls crowded between Jed and me so they could look out the front windshield to see what was happening. We saw him enter the Pizza Place, and we waited for him to exit the establishment.

"What's taking him so long?" asked Ellen.

"I guess he is waiting for closing time," I suggested.

"When does that place close?" asked Emily.

"About now, I think," I said and glanced at my watch. "It's after 9 pm now, so he should be leaving pretty soon."

I was correct. I saw the young man exit the Pizza Place and stand in front of the door. It appeared that he was surveying the parking lot. The delivery car was right where he had parked it.

There was one other car in the lot, and I assumed that vehicle belonged to the night manager, who was in the process of cleaning up and closing.

The young man walked to the delivery car, removed the Pizza Place sign from the rooftop, and re-entered the establishment.

"Why did he do that?" asked Ellen.

"It's not his sign. Someone will have to use it for deliveries tomorrow," I guessed.

We waited some more.

My cell phone rang, startling me again. My nerves were so very on edge.

"Hello?" I said after glancing at the caller ID.

"Lindsay Harris, please," said the smug-sounding voice.

"You've got her," I answered just as smugly.

"I suppose you are watching me and waiting for me to leave," he said in a strong, self-assured tone.

"Actually, I'm at the drugstore buying feminine items for all of the ladies of my house," I explained.

"Is that what you told those cops sitting in your kitchen?" he asked.

"Sure, that is exactly what I told them," I said as I glanced at Jed.

"Did they believe you?" he asked.

"Of course, because it is the truth," I said defensively. It really was the truth because I had stopped on the way to the stakeout to pick up some items so it would not be a bold-faced lie. I wanted to walk into the house with bags clutched in my hands filled with products from the drugstore.

"I didn't see you anywhere, but I know you're watching me. I can feel it in my bones," he said eerily.

"You're feeling guilt, that's all. Now, when can I have Ryan?" I asked harshly.

"If I catch one single glimpse of you or your car, you will never see your son again," he said as he disconnected the line.

I sucked in a deep breath, held it for a few moments, and then exhaled.

I told Jed and the girls what Brian had said. I did not panic. We continued to watch and wait for him to leave the Pizza Place.

An hour later, he finally walked out of the door. Again, he looked around to see if he could spot us. I don't think he even glanced at the hill across the street from him, and I was so was grateful.

Chapter 22

"Jed, I think we have to follow him. I think he plans to kill Ryan regardless of what I say or do," I said angrily.

"I think you're right, Linds," he replied.

"Girls, you need to sit back and fasten your seat-belts. We might be in for a long night," I said sternly.

Brian White started his car and let it idle for several minutes before reversing from the parking space and heading for the road.

I let my car sit, not running it because I knew as soon as I put the car into gear, the headlights would pop on, alerting him where we were lying in wait. We watched him drive across the road and head up the incline that would take him to the mall, which was directly past the bank behind where we were hiding.

Still, I did not start the car.

"Let's go," said Jed.

"No, we need to see if he is going to go on his way or just continue to search for us. The headlights are a dead giveaway. I can't start the car. Not yet," I explained.

I could hear the girls fidgeting in the back seat. I assumed they were getting a little worried about their part in this whole scenario.

"He's coming back this way. Everybody ducked down so he can't see us," I instructed. We could see the beams from his headlights shine through the car.

"He can see us, Mom," whispered Ellen.

"No, he can't if you ducked down as far as you can. He is actually too far away from us to see anything below the window.

"He's getting closer," whispered Emily.

"Just stay down," I cautioned.

When the light disappeared, I popped my head up barely enough to see where he was headed. He was going back down the incline. He must have thought he had scared us away from the idea of following him. As soon as he made a right turn onto the road in front of us, I started the car and moved along fast enough to catch sight of him. I memorized the shape of his taillights and backed off as far as I thought I could so he wouldn't guess that we were on his tail.

"Mom, you're going to lose him," whispered Ellen.

"I hope not," I replied with a steady gaze on the road before me.

I was staying far enough away from his car so that I would totally lose sight of him each time we rounded a curve. But, by the same token, he would lose sight of us, too. I just prayed that he wouldn't think he was being followed.

"What are we going to do when we catch up to him at his house?" asked Emily.

"Well, Jed and I will get out and go after him. You guys will have to stay in the car. I don't want either of you to get hurt," I said in a motherly 'no questions asked' tone.

"I've lost him, Jed. I think he turned off just ahead," I said with concern.

I slowed to a crawl; Jed looked to the right, and I looked left searching for the taillights.

"There. Over there," I said. I pointed to my left at taillights that had just flashed off.

"I need to drive on by, turn around up ahead, and drive back close enough for us to get out of the car without being seen. That is going to be hard to do in the blackness of the night. It will be hard to do when I have no control over the headlights after I put the car into drive."

"Yeah, some of the safety devices on cars make it hard to be a stalker," said Jed trying hard to make us laugh to break the heavy tension filling the car.

"We're not stalkers," said Ellen defensively.

"That's the only thing you can call it," said Jed.

"No, we're brother-hunting," said Emily.

"Okay, okay, I stand corrected," said Jed.

"Jed, I'm pulling over right here. We'll get out and walk to his house. Girls, keep the doors locked while we're gone. You keep my cell phone, and if we aren't back in thirty minutes, call the police. All you need to do is punch 9-1-1, okay?" I asked.

"Mom, we should go with you," said Ellen.

"No, we need someone to call for help if we need it," I explained. "Nobody knows we're here or what we're doing."

"I'm scared, Mom," said Emily in a timid, little girl's voice.

"I am, too, but Jed and I have to do this," I said as I tried to reassure her.

Chapter 23

We exited the car as quickly as possible so that the interior light would shine for only a few seconds.

Jed and I started walking toward a long driveway a few hundred yards ahead of us. We stayed as close as we possibly could to the high weeds and trees that lined the way. It was difficult to do. Without a light of some kind, we couldn't see hidden holes in the ground that could trip us and possibly cause us to fall and break an ankle.

We reached the driveway and ducked down as low as possible as we walked so we would be hard to spot.

The house was well-lit all the way around and that was going to make it even harder to get close enough to look inside and locate Ryan.

Suddenly the front door opened. I held my breath. I was sure Jed did the same thing. A figure stepped outside the front door and looked around from side to side.

Jed and I plopped down on the cold, wet grass so he couldn't see us. At least, we hoped and prayed that he couldn't see us. We heard the door close. Jed looked up to see if he had gone back inside.

"All clear," he whispered softly.

We both got to our knees, then to our feet, so we could continue our hunched-over walk to get closer to the house.

"That was close," I whispered. I struggled to get my breath to return to normal again. "I'm going to the right," I whispered. "You go to the left so he won't be able to catch us both at the same time. At least not until we meet on the other side."

"Are you all right?" asked Jed.

"Yeah, just scared for us and Ryan," I said with rasps tinting my words.

"We can do this," said Jed, but his encouragement was fading.

Jed ran across the front of the house to get to the left side while I inched forward. I was in an area with less coverage. If anyone was going to be spotted, it was going to be me.

I didn't think Brian White had any accomplices, since the two who had helped with the robbery of the grocery store were in jail. I wasn't afraid anyone would sneak up behind me. All of the action I was going to see or confront would be directly in front of me.

I was wrong.

I heard a gunshot to my left.

Oh no! Jed! I screamed to myself. I started to jump up and run to help him. I reconsidered and thought again. *I should stay put for a few moments and start inching forward again.*

I heard a moan, and I cursed myself for not running to Jed's aid. Then, there was a large commotion. It sounded like some kind of animal fight was happening on the left side of the house. This time, I had to go see. I jumped up, putting myself in the open, and ran toward the noise. I saw Jed and Brian White grappling and fighting each other. I quickly ran inside the house to find Ryan.

I looked into each of the small rooms, but I couldn't find him. I looked inside closets and under beds. There was no sign of him.

Please, God, I prayed, *help me find my baby.*

I walked into the kitchen and looked inside cabinets. I looked under the counters. No luck. I had stepped forward and walked toward the back door. I felt the floor sag a bit. I looked down and saw a sunken handle in the floor board. This meant that there was a basement.

I could still hear the two men fighting outside. I yanked hard on the door and pulled it up.

"Mom! Get me out of here!" shouted Ryan. His voice came from a small room about the size of a walk-in closet.

I saw a step ladder leaning against the wall. I picked it up and hauled it to the opened door in the floor. I lowered the ladder down to Ryan.

"Open it up and climb out of there, baby," I said as I held back tears.

Ryan was up the ladder and into my arms in no time. I clung to him with all of my strength.

"I knew you would find me," cried Ryan.

Suddenly, I heard sirens, lots of sirens. The girls must have called the police since it had taken us longer than the half hour to find Ryan.

Out of the corner of my eye, I saw Jed appear at the back door. He was beaten and bloody. I didn't see a bullet wound, so I assumed the first shot had missed him and that the moan had been a decoy.

I ran over to him and helped him walk inside the house.

All three of us—Ryan, Jed, and I—walked through the small house to the front door. We opened the door wide, walked out to the porch, and stood together pushing our clasped hands into the air.

We were met by the girls, who were running up the driveway toward us.

The police officers found Brian White lying in a painful heap at the side of the house. They handcuffed Brian and pushed him into the back of the police car.

I realized how devious Brian White had been to lure Ryan away from me. Brian White realized how devious I had been when I had discovered his identity and lured him into making moves so I could follow him.

After talking to the detectives who had been investigating Ryan's kidnapping, the five of us climbed into the car and headed for home. I needed to call Justin to let him know that we had gotten Ryan back home safe and sound.

We were all tired but very happy.

I had discovered that *Snooping Can Be Devious*.

ABOUT THE AUTHOR

Linda Hudson Hoagland of Tazewell, Virginia, graduated from Southwest Virginia Community College and has won numerous awards for her novels, short stories, essays, and poems. Many of her works have been published in anthologies, including *Cup of Comfort*. Other publications include nine mystery novels, six nonfiction books, a collection of short stories, and a volume of poetry.

Coming Soon

Volume four in the
Lindsay Harris Murder Mystery Series
goes to the dogs when Lindsay and her
friend, Annie, search for the reason
that Annie's dog was murdered.